THE

TURTLE

AND OTHER STORIES

D. L. GILMORE

D. L. GILMORE

ISBN: 0692298746

ISBN-13: 978-0692298749 (Ulinawi Works)

FOR SUSAN

CONTENTS

FORWARD

I am a Southerner. I start with that because it helps to explain the characters in this book. The South is rather famous for its quirky characters. Southern writers far better than I have paid their rent by writing about their neighbors and family members. In the television comedy series "Designing Women," the character Julia Sugarbaker summed up the South and our people:

I'm saying this is the South. And we're proud of our crazy people. We don't hide them up in the attic. We bring 'em right down to the living room and show 'em off. See... no one in the South ever asks if you have crazy people in your family. They just ask what side they're on.

Quirkiness is not monopolized by the South. Every one of us, regardless of our nationality, race, sectionality, creed, religion, sex, or clan has quirky, sometimes strange, crazy people in our lives. If we're lucky, maybe the crazy people are our friends. I heard a fella say that one of out five people is crazy and if you are really careful and select four perfectly sane friends, then look in the mirror. The crazy person is staring back at you.

This book is not about fly fishing, although it has fly fishing in it. It is about book about friends and community and family and growing up and watching your kids grow up and living. If you are a fly fisherman and want a technical treatise of fishing, go buy Vince Marinaro's <u>A Dry Fly Code</u>. If you are not a fisherman, I think you'll still find some things in these pages that might appeal to you. I hope so, at any rate.

The Turtle stories were previously published on-line on the now defunct Virtual Fly Shop website. The remaining stories are either published for the first time here or were published on-line on the *FlyAnglers.Org* website. One story, *The Lucky One*, was previously published in *Fish and Fly Magazine* with rights retained by me.

I particularly need to thank my wife, Susan, and my children: Brad, Jess, and Tyler. I cannot think of words sufficient to express how lucky I am to have them.

I thank my brothers Dwight, Matt, and Mark and my sister, Dianne. They are my family. Some of these stories have parts of them woven in their fabric.

I thank Ronnie Hall for hours in duck blinds and in drift boats and sharing with me the unusual philosophies that can arise when Single Malt Whisky is poured after long days in the out-of-doors. Ronnie was the first guide to put a driftboat on the Hiwassee River in Southeast Tennessee. These days you can find him doing less strenuous work at The Fish Hawk Fly Fishing store in Atlanta, Georgia.

I thank my friend Don Gibson. Don owns a cabin located on some of the best and most difficult trout water in this country. He has been gracious enough to share that water with me, along with a memorable trip to Alaska where we chased fish and dodged half ton grizzly bears and walked miles in soft tundra surrounded by heaven on earth.

I should mention Mike Delp, a retired creative writing teacher up in the great fishing paradise that is Michigan, well north of that Detroit business. Mike bugged me to publish these stories, gave me some helpful criticism about character descriptions and occasionally chewed my butt for not moving quicker. I don't know why. It only took me fifteen years to publish these.

I thank Colston Newton and Mark Wendt: boys, we have had a run, haven't we? I thank James Moore in Arkansas – James, you'll recognize your story.

I thank Commander Joel Stewart (US Navy) for his contributions to all of our freedoms. Joel is an avid outdoorsman and fly angler. While he was in Baghdad immediately after the fall of Saddam Hussein, he started a fly fishing school to teach soldiers, marines and sailors how to fly fish during their downtime. He asked Edward Laine and I to help him with equipment. Ed spearheaded the effort and we ended up sending a ton of fishing equipment over to Iraq. Rick Pope, founder of Temple Fork Outfitters, sent dozens of fly rods just because we asked him and because he wanted to help Joel and our troops. The pictures of soldiers and marines in uniform, M-4 rifles slung across their backs, with fly rods in their hands and sometimes fish, are still etched in my mind. Joel's written and published a book about his adventure titled <u>A Fly Rod in My Sea Bag</u> that's available through Amazon.

I want to thank my friends that are members of an internet fly fishing club called "The Gathering of the Clan." We get together once a year to fish and socialize and to raise money for *Project Healing Waters*. PHW is a charity that works with wounded veterans to provide opportunities and access to fly fishing. You can learn more about Project Healing Waters at *www.projecthealingwaters.org*

I thank my good friend Lieutenant Colonel Edward Patrick Kelleher, formerly of Pacific Grove, California. Ed encouraged me and pressed me to publish these stories. I regret that they were not published before he passed away. Colonel Kelleher was an inspiration and friend to my oldest son, Brad. Ed delayed his cancer treatment so he could fly from California to Georgia to attend Brad's wedding. Ed and I were soldiers once, and young. Sir, I miss you.

I thank Fred Bridge of York, Pennsylvania for his friendship over the years. Fred was the greatest junk fly fisherman I've known. He's fishing in Heaven's Jordan now. I miss hearing his whooping and hollering when he caught a fish, acting like a kid every time.

Carl DeFazio of Romney, West Virginia provided the cover art. Carl is the world's only Amish Catholic and is a great photographer of nature. Carl, thank you so much for your generosity in sharing your gift with me. You can see more of Carl's work, visit his website at *www.mountaineerflies.com*.

My good friend Edward W. Laine served as editor and proof-reader of this book. I have great difficulty editing my own writing and Ed volunteered to try to expunge my typos, comma splices, and other troubles. I am sure that there are still problems, especially my personal sin: the comma splice, which will give English teachers pause to pull out blue pencils. Edward and I are brothers really. He's a bit more experienced in years than I, but we bonded a long time ago over single malt scotch, fly fishing, good literature, good manners, and an appreciation for sarcasm. Edward, thank you for being my friend.

Lastly, I want to thank you for taking the time to read these stories. I assure you that while there are moments of fancy, not a small number of the events described did actually happen. The names and places may have been changed to protect the perpetrators.

Doug Gilmore
30 September 2014

Every man looks at his own wood-pile
with a kind of affection.
-Henry David Thoreau, *Walden*

However rare true love may be,
it is less so than true friendship.

- ALBERT EINSTEIN

We live ... in a world starved for
solitude, silence, and private:
and therefore starved for meditation
and true friendship.
-   C.S. LEWIS, <u>The Weight of Glory</u>
-

THE TURTLE

EUGENE "TURTLE" WALLACE is my friend. Despite his nickname, Turtle is not slow, he is not quiet, and he does not live in a shell. Sometimes I think he lives at my house. He shows up whenever the mood strikes him.

The fall after Turtle's second wife left him, the mood struck him at least every other day. Most of Turtle's visits then were the sort I would have preferred to escape. He would sit on the front porch of our house in one of our white wicker-wrapped rockers and stare out across the grass of our front lawn that slopes down to the rhododendron-flanked creek that separates our property from the county road below us. If he came before noon, he would sit in the rocker, with a cup of coffee in his left hand and a Marlboro in his right hand. After the noon hour, he'd switch the coffee for Budweiser and keep the Marlboro going. For weeks, the pattern repeated itself. Turtle believed that he had house rights, or "rats" as he would pronounce it.

One morning shortly after the kids had left for school, I heard gravel crunching in the driveway and the familiar rattling of Turtle's ancient pickup truck. I walked in the kitchen and waited for Turtle to slam the truck door. Then I counted to four. At the four count, I opened the kitchen door and stood aside as Turtle barged in.

Turtle was excited: so excited that he picked Dani up by

her waist and twirled her like a cheerleader.

"For gracious sakes, Eugene - put me down!"

My wife calls Turtle by his Christian name. Turtle doesn't care for it much – mostly because he was tormented when he was little by playground bullies for being named "Eugene," a name that doesn't scream masculinity and toughness like Chuck or Hank or Jack. Turtle grew up in junior high, outgrew his tormentors and had his revenge with each one of them. No one calls Turtle by his given name now except for Dani and a few silver-haired matrons in our county.

"I'm sorry Dani. Jack, you gotta come with me. You gotta come. I have done seen heaven and it's rat here in Cherohowla County!"

"What in blazes are you talking about, Turtle?"

Turtle is known for his flights of fancy – has been since we were in high school together and he was convinced that he was the illegitimate son of Patsy Cline and Jerry Lee Lewis, despite his daddy then being the sheriff of our county. One day he'd walk around singing, as loud as he could: *You shake my nerve and you rattle my brain, too much love drive's a man insane.* The next day, he'd be singing *Crazy... Crazy for feeling so lonely, I'm crazy. Crazy for feeling blue.* Now that I think about it, maybe he was more right than I had thought.

"Jack, you know that place up 'air near Sharon's Mountain? Where Jerry Bob found them likker makers?"

"Yes, I know the place."

Jerry Bob Whitestone had been a classmate of ours at

Cherohowla High School. He went off to college at Vanderbilt University and then on to the Marines. I went to Georgia Tech and then to the Army. Turtle went off to....well Turtle didn't go to college. He got Mary Beth Haymaker pregnant and her father, the Right Honorable Judge Horace Horatio Haymaker IV, put a Winchester Model 21 to Turtle's nose and married the two of them right there in the Judge's living room. Turtle's promise as a running back for the University of Tennessee was done. Judge Haymaker, besides being our superior court judge, was also the chairman of our Draft Board.   Three weeks after the wedding, a proper amount of time for the newlyweds to have a honeymoon and settle into their lives together, Turtle received his draft notice. Two weeks later, Turtle took a long bus ride to Fort Polk, Louisiana to begin his education in the ways of the United States Army and infantry training. Turtle apparently rather enjoyed the Army and reenlisted after his two-year draft obligation hitch. By the time Jerry Bob and I graduated from college and were shipped to Vietnam, Turtle was on his voluntary third tour, having become an Army Ranger. In its bureaucratic wisdom, the Army assigned me as the platoon leader over Turtle's platoon.

Jerry Bob spent his thirteen months in Vietnam as a Marine. Then, after his time was up, he got out and came home to Cherohowla County, ran for Sheriff and won. He then managed to get himself murdered on his second week on the job after stumbling upon the wrong set of moonshiners up on Sharon's Mountain. He killed the three rotgut makers before dying of his wounds. He became the hero in death to the law-abiding citizens of Cherohowla County that Turtle and I had known Jerry Bob to be.

Turtle finally came home from Vietnam after five years in the Army and three tours outside the wire. He managed to stay married to Mary Beth for a year after coming home, before she kicked him out. His second wife was more pleasant than Mary Beth. She didn't kick Turtle out. She left.

"You ain't gonna believe what I saw this mornin'! I was up 'air, lookin' for a stand of walnut I'd heard about," Turtle made his living logging fine wood for custom furniture builders in Atlanta, Charlotte, Chattanooga and Greenville. "Albert at the feed store in Ridgeville told me about this big stand of walnut back of Sharon's Mountain Primitive Baptist Church."

"Okay."

"Beavers got back in the holler behind the Baptist Church. So I sneak off up there yesterday and holey moley, you ain't gonna believe the specks that fill that water. It looks like a bunch of fish tanks at a hatchery. There's specks as big as any I've seen since them sumbitches Howard Baker and Jimmy Carter dammed up the Little Tenn."

Dani scolded him for cursing. Turtle dropped his head and then looked out of the window, looking towards the trees on the other side of the lawn. And then he apologized. Apologies don't come easy to Turtle, but he knew better than to take on Dani.

Turtle was prone to exaggeration to be sure, but the idea that brook trout (speckled trout, or specks, in mountain parlance) had taken up residence behind the Sharon's Mountain Primitive Baptist Church was something else altogether. Turtle and I had fished since the mid-60's. The Little Tennessee had been our favorite water, regularly yielding brookies in the fourteen to eighteen-inch category. But TVA decided that a dam would look better than the best water in the South and Senator Howard Baker and President Jimmy Carter made sure they got the money. Turtle never forgave them for that. Me neither.

The next morning Turtle was on my doorstep at five a.m. tapping out a song with his antsy feet while I grabbed the rod tube and my ditty bag. We drove the hour drive over Hogback Ridge, down through the valley, and then up the winding dirt road that leads to the Sharon's Mountain Primitive Baptist Church, a place where foot-washin' still happens every Sunday and home to the only Baptists I know who drink wine with communion. They are also the only white Baptists I know that admit to dancing.

The walk up the hollow behind the church and beyond the walnut grove was not an easy stroll. The trees in the hollow were predominately old-growth poplars and the snowstorm in '93 had laid down trees with trunks the size of small cars. This had been the only area in Cherohowla County not to have been timbered out in the late 1800's. Some those trees had been standing when Longstreet chased Yankees up and down the western spine of the Appalachians after Chickamauga.

What would have been a one-mile walk turned out to be more like two as we climbed over, around, and under trees that a lumberman's dreams are made of. Turtle would have given his left arm to make lumber out of those trees and had said so, but the church members that owned the land would not give him permission.

Winded and sweating, we eventually made it through the windfalls and were standing directly downstream of the first beaver dam. Turtle reached in his pocket and pulled out a pack of Marlboros, offering me one. I took it. I reached in my ditty bag and offered him the flask – he drank from it and handed it back.

"I figure we'll just belly crawl up to the dam and cast upstream," Turtle offered. "Them specks might be pooled at the dam, so we gotta stay back some and cast off our knees, else they'll see us."

I knew what Turtle would fish. He most often fishes a Yallerhammer, no matter when, where or what time of year. I know for a fact that he still uses authentic feathers regardless of what the game boys say or how many times I try to teach him that killing a member of an endangered species like the Yellow Flicker, aka Yallerhammer, is not a good thing.

"Oh hell Jack: that damned yeller woodpecker ain't endangered, 'cept the ones that come and peck on my house. Shit, we got more yeller flickers in Wilson holler than them DNR boys says are alive in the world."

"Turtle, that may be, but you need to realize that if people keep shooting yellow flickers, pretty soon there won't be any flickers down at Wilson's."

"Phhht...you done gone crazy and joined them tree-huggin' college commies."

Our conversations go like that. I try to drag him into the

21st Century. Turtle tries to retreat into the 19th and we end up somewhere in the 20th, hopefully in the latter part, at least environmentally. In the meantime, any flicker in Wilson Holler that pecks on Turtle's house is likely to end up tied up into little dingy feathered flies, thrown from Turtle's 80-year-old Granger. Turtle's grandfather had left him his entire collection of Grangers. Turtle has never fished with anything but bamboo. He may be borderline white trash, but he is white trash with good taste. There had been one E.F. Payne in the lot, a six and a half foot beauty that throws a five weight double taper line effortlessly. Turtle gave me the Payne one night: said it didn't fit with the four Grangers in the set.

By seven-thirty, we were rigged up and crawling to the dam. I nodded to Turtle – he'd have first honors. On his knees, bending forward slightly at the waist, Turtle made one false cast and the fly line shot out forty feet, landing like air on the water with the fly dropping and sinking, ever so slowly. He stripped one inch and raised the rod. I watched as the rod bent in the graceful arc, extending well back towards Turtle's hand, the muscular power of the fish transmitted through the line to the rod to the wrist and into the forearm of my friend. The brookie came exploding upwards, tail-walking and Turtle dropped the rod tip to the side, keeping tension on the tippet. He cursed, hoping the fish wouldn't spook the others. In a minute, he slid his net under the speck and lifted it over the dam.

The brookie was easily a dozen inches long with a girth that told of too many lazy afternoons eating rising mayflies and fallen inchworms. It was a beautiful fish.

Turtle grinned and raised his hand for the high five that he demanded after such feats. I obliged and the trout was allowed to slip back out of the net and swim back to its friends in the pool. One of the proudest moments of my life was the day that Turtle finally accepted that he could release trout instead of eating everything he caught. It took me five years and too many arguments to get him to listen. Now we may keep one each for lunch, but that's it. It was still too early in the morning for lunch, so anything we caught then would be sent home to its kin.

It was now my turn at the pool of specks. I am not half the caster Turtle is, but I managed to toss a #14 Tellico so that it landed about fifteen feet to the right of where Turtle's earlier cast had been. It started its slow descent into the water and then, at the point where the tippet was submerged and the leader broke the water's surface, I saw the tell-tale twitch that told me Mr. Speckled Brook Trout had come to dinner. I set the hook. We had a lovely time for about thirty seconds before I landed and released a beautiful hen, puffed up and ready to lay. The fish's flanks were olive green, spotted with narrow golden squiggles near its spine, transitioning further down its sides to occasional blue rimmed reddish miniature moons interspersed with tiny rounded golden suns, giving way to a belly of red orange above ivory - the promise of regeneration.

We both caught two more each out of that pool. They were easy trout, not yet driven to cynicism by the offerings of humans: no selectivity, just opportunists - the way trout had been for a million years before man started trying to deceive them with handmade bundles of fur and feathers. Trout are like people. They start off naïve and innocent, eager to explore and taste the world around them. Then somewhere along the line, they feel the sharp pain of deceit and it hardens them and makes them mistrusting, dour, and crotchety. I have fished too many years for trout with attitudes.

We left that pool and walked on upstream, skirting the boggy edge of the beaver pool. It was obvious why the brookies were in such good shape and of such good size. There were freshets of water seeping from springs that flowed out of limestone at temperatures low enough to defeat the high temperatures of August.

About a hundred yards upstream was the second pool. It was smaller than the first, but the beavers had managed to clear enough trees around it that the sun had full access to over half the pond surface. We could see dimples as the brookies ate breakfast the easy way, on the surface.

Turtle bent low and sent a cast curling towards a slight bulge in the smooth water surface, indicating a large trout cruising for emergers. The fly settled into the water's film and Turtle stripped the Yallerhammer slightly: short strip, let it settle, short strip, let it settle, and so on - three casts and nothing. Cursing at me when I reminded him that the Yallerhammer, while a great fly, is not always the best fly, he cast a fourth time. I joked that this was his lunch cast, so he'd better catch something or he'd be eating nothing but watercress for lunch.

"Bite me," he replied.

That's when it hit and hit hard, nearly ripping the rod from Turtle's hand - bending it almost double, see-sawing back and forth, pulsing with pure kinetic energy, threatening with each surge to break the slender rod.

"Oh man what a trout!"

"Turtle, that's not a trout!"

"'Course it's a trout! What the hell else would it be?"

"You hooked a beaver."

"Shit."

Turtle stood and started trying to turn the beaver. I told him to break it off. But Turtle wasn't having it. He had it in his mind to catch the water rat.

The beaver swam upstream, looking for home. Line was being ripped from the reel and it was only a matter of time before the tippet broke or Turtle ran out of line. He handed me the rod and demanded:

"Don't lose that fish!"

He dove over the beaver dam and started swimming after the beaver. He swam through the deep pool with long strokes, pushing water beside him, boring forward with his head down, only coming up for air every third stroke.

The beaver turned. I stripped line back in as fast as I could pull. I looked up and saw the beaver and Turtle were headed straight for each other, oblivious to the other, each intent on their own purpose – the beaver to be shed of the hook embedded in his side, and Turtle, determined that the beaver not get away. I was trying not to laugh and to strip line at the same time. The beaver and the Turtle were headed on a collision course.

The deep water turned shallow and Turtle stood up, straight up, with the water at his waist. The beaver was twenty feet in front of him, still coming, me still stripping line to keep the line from going slack. The beaver was a kamikaze, bent on destruction.

And then the beaver stopped, realizing that the large mass in front of him was a danger. Turtle pounced.

There are amazing sights that a man ought to see before he dies and fishes the native trout stream that is the Heavenly Jordan: the Katmai in Alaska from a de Havilland Beaver, the sun appearing over the rim from the bottom of the Grand Canyon, the birth of his children, the smile on his wife's face when he's finally done something that made her happy. But the sight that was more wondrous, more rare, and more utterly ridiculous than any before was the sight that morning of Eugene "Turtle" Wallace wrestling a beaver in a forest pool two miles up and half a world away from the Sharon's Mountain Primitive Baptist Church.

We had watercress salad for lunch, sitting beside a small fire that I built to help Turtle dry out. That was a sight too – Turtle naked as a jaybird, clothes strung over every rhododendron in sight, bandage on his left hand where the beaver had clawed him, just before the beaver got away, a fugitive from Turtle's justice. Turtle looked like death itself – his torso pallid from never seeing the sun, blood oozing from deep scratches on his face and chest, and traces of mud still streaking his lower half.

"You think you learned anything today?" I asked as I took another sip from the flask and inhaled the cigarette that I should not have been enjoying.

"Hell, yes. I learn't that you ain't worth a fiddler's fart at keepin' tension on a fly rod. If you'd a kept that beaver's head up, I'd 've caught him and we'd now be eatin' beaver 'stead of this blasted muskrat weed. What did you learn, smart ass?"

"I learned how ridiculous a naked Turtle looks.....and I learned that given the right environment, a beaver will whip a Turtle's ass any day of the week. I also learned that you've screwed up the fishing in this pool for a long while."

"Shoot," Turtle said, spitting a stream of Copenhagen and saliva at the fire. "Wait 'til next week. There's a place over near them Kilmer trees where the bears are as thick as ants in honey. We'll go there next week and have some real fun!'"

For Colston

THE TURTLE AND THE FOX

HUMANS IN SOUTHERN APPALACHIA are a relatively recent phenomenon according to the archaeology folks up in Knoxville. The American Indian explored and populated large segments of western North America and filled up the continent of South America long before he settled in the green mountains of that line the Blue Ridge.

White men, of course, came even later: as late as the 1820's in some corners of Georgia. They drove out the Cherokee (who, in their own ethnocide, had driven out and slaughtered the Creek) during the 1830's. Cherohowla County, my home, was formed from land "liberated" - *sarcasm intended* - from the red man. Cherohowla once comprised an area large enough that the old boys down at the state legislature decided in the 1850's to divide it into two different counties: Cherohowla and Tyler (in honor of the former president). Rosemary is the county seat for Cherohowla. Clarkstown is the seat of Tyler County. They are divided by the highest mountain south of the Smokies; a craggy, shaggy animal of rock and earth and trees and right angles and rushing waters called Cagle's Knob.

The entire area around here was settled almost exclusively by a race of men and women known as the Ulster Scots. They were Scots whom the great king, James of England (the same guy who had the King James Bible published) evicted from their own homes in Scotland so he could give some more land to his English buddies. He sent them to take over Northern Ireland to piss off the Pope and the Irish and to get them out of his hair. They did not care for this arrangement. The more ambitious climbed on boats and came to America in the 1600's. They settled in and around Lancaster County, Pennsylvania. Eventually, they fanned out up and down the spine of the Blue Ridge with its green mountains and hills that reminded them so much of home - only with better weather. They were an obstinate lot, given to long memories, short tempers, and strong opinions. Their descendants retain these traits.

In 1861, a group of hotheads and malcontents from the oft-maligned and never understood independent planet of South Carolina decided to shoot at a few soldiers who were sweating in the mid-day sun on a sunny island off Charleston. A bunch of other hotheads decided to join in with them, starting a little thing called "The War Between The States". It wasn't the first time the South Carolinians had stirred up a pot of evil stew – they'd tried something similar in the 1830's but the great Indian Murderer and sometime lawyer Andrew Jackson had conned his way into the White House. Old Hickory, who had no problem exercising power, turned his malice towards the South Carolinian politicos and told he would arrest them and have them shot if they didn't shut up. It worked. But nearly thirty years later Lincoln did not have the cajones of Jackson. So we had ourselves a little war that ended up killing 600,000 Americans, give or take a few ten thousands.

Rosemary and its over-mountain neighbor, Clarkstown, took different sides in the war. There is some disagreement some 140 years later as to why, but I think it was mostly because Cherohowla had a grand total of seven slaves, all owned by the same fellow who no one liked anyway. Tyler County, on the other hand, mostly because it was home to two broad valleys that were prime agricultural spots, had over 100 slaves and a dozen or so slaveholders. The folks of Cherohowla didn't want any part of fighting a war to protect human property and rich folks so they sided with the North.

The Tyler folks, being unduly influenced by a couple of well-spoken slave-holding preachers and the usual riff-raff of bankers, lawyers, and tax men, threw their lot in with the boys in Gray. To be sure, there were Cherohowla boys in gray and Tyler boys in blue (all the Southern Appalachians from western Virginia to northern Alabama and Georgia were similarly afflicted), but the bulk of folk from each county sided as I have said. Of course this created a litany of problems for the accursed Braxton Bragg, Commander of the Army of Tennessee, as he first moved up the spine and then tucked tail and ran south to Georgia where Sherman sent him packing.

When it was over the animosities really started to build. Lee may have surrendered at Appomattox and Davis may have been found in middle Georgia, trying to get away to Cuba, but the war never ended between Cherohowla and Tyler. Maybe one of these days when all these damn folks who keep moving up here from the cities outnumber us native folk, then the hatchet will be buried - but not until then.

Back during that abomination called Reconstruction, folks were actually shot and marauding miscreants burned homes in both counties. Later during the twenties, when football was introduced to the local school systems, the war moved to the football field and the soldiers were the players from Cherohowla High School and its arch-rival, Tyler High School.

From 1928 until 1932 the Tyler High Rebels won four consecutive state championships while the Cherohowla Patriots suffered. In 1932 after enduring four years of humiliation and noticing that they were down by 3 touchdowns before half time, the Cherohowla faithful decided enough was enough. When the fighting was over most of the players on both teams had broken something and most of the men were at least bleeding (the women were safe; it was a more "genteel" time). As a result both teams were disbanded until after World War II had been fought and won - both counties fought on the same side in that one. In the spirit of post-war brotherhood the rivalry was restarted. Although it was less bloody, it was no less intense.

In 1967 Eugene "Turtle" Wallace, Jerry Bob Whitestone, and myself were seniors at Cherohowla High. Turtle was the starting halfback for the Patriots. Jerry Bob was the first black quarterback in Cherohowla history. I blocked for both guys as fullback and, on the other side of the ball, as weak-side linebacker. Jerry was strong, Turtle - middle. We had not lost a game all year. We had not been scored on. We were the best team in the state. We had already beaten the Tyler Rebs by twenty-seven points during the regular season. Sent their tired butts home to wallow in their self-pity. But they managed to make it through their half of the state playoff bracket. We met at the state capital in December 1967 to play for the State Championship.

They came ready. Before the game, someone managed to get into our locker room and salted all the jockstraps with "Atom Bomb", the strongest analgesic cream known at that time. It made Maximum Strength Ben-Gay seem like toothpaste. For a full half, we cried in pain and watched Tyler go up 14-0. At halftime, we looked at blisters and every man jack there knew none of us would father a child. That was later proven wrong, particularly by our center Junior McTiernan who would father 8 children he admitted to *before* he met those Mormon kids on their bicycles. But we were convinced of eternal impotence at the time.

By the end of the third quarter, Tyler was up 28 to 3 and it seemed hopeless. Fans were leaving the stadium. Our coach, Elijah Solomon McManus, had been kicked out of the game and was sitting in his car outside the stadium, surrounded by State Troopers. I was in tears.

That's when Turtle got mad, not just mad, but genuinely, completely she-bear angry mad.

Third and two on our seventeen yard line: Tyler has the ball and is about to score yet again. Tyler's QB, Fox Murphy, takes the ball on a bootleg left. Turtle throws the blocking back to the ground and hits Fox so hard that people groan in the stands. I pick up the fumble and run eighty yards to score the only touchdown of my high school career. But of course, there was a whistle and a penalty because as every idiot knew, you couldn't advance a fumble in high school ball back then. Delay of Game. Ball on our own 12. Jerry Bob keeps the ball off the split option and runs 88 yards to glory. Seven minutes later, mostly because Eugene "Turtle" Wallace lost his mind and all his reservations and scored three touchdowns in seven minutes, we completed the greatest comeback in state playoff history.

I was thinking about this the day I read the Rosemary News and Gazette's lead story about the planned development of Cagle's Knob.

CAGLE'S KNOB TO BE RESORT!!!

The headline was above an article that told of how our old nemesis Edward G. "Fox" Murphy was pleased to announce that his company, Murphy Properties, LLC, had negotiated to purchase Cagle's Knob and its environs. He would be developing "a high-end residential development for urban investors who wished to share the unique beauty and peace of the surrounding nature."

I finished the article just in time to see (and hear) Turtle's truck tearing up my driveway, tossing what little gravel was left out of the driveway and into the surrounding grass.

"That sumbitch!!! I'm gonna kill 'im. I shoulda kilt him years ago, but I didn't."

Turtle screamed through his opened window, not waiting until the truck stopped before he opened the door and jumped out of the truck. This is a recurring habit of Turtle when he is really upset. The problem is that my driveway is quite steep next to the house and on more than one occasion, Turtle has done his rolling exit and then discovered his truck rolling backwards downhill towards Dani's flower garden. Most times he catches his truck. But sometimes he hasn't and then he has to get down on his knees and replant, resow, and repair Dani's flowers ... or risk emasculation or worse.

"Turtle, put the blasted brake on. I read the article. Shut up and see to your truck before you get Dani going," I instructed.

Too late: Dani had heard the commotion and following the old adage about there not being any knowledge as fixed as that gained through experience, opened the door and scolded Turtle.

"Eugene Wallace, if that truck rolls into my flowers one more time...",

"Dani, you might want to read this while Turtle tends to his truck." I handed her the paper.

"Oh, my stars!" She slumped in the chair and stared out at the yard, face blank, stunned.

Turtle broke the silence.

"He is a lowdown lyin', cheatin', sorry as sin piece of trash, and I'm gonna finally teach him that lesson he's been needin' for too long."

The problems were as deep as the Civil War and as clear-cut as the forest would be once Murphy turned his chain saws and bulldozers loose on the oaks and poplars and hickories and laurel and rhododendron on Cagle's Knob.

Murphy had built a reputation in Atlanta of building strip shopping centers and high-density, low price houses. Wanting to "return to his roots," he'd moved back to Tyler

County and predictably returned with his "cut all the trees down, plow up all the topsoil, build ugly buildings and then plant Bradford Pears and call it green" mentality intact. That was enough in itself to make both Turtle and I dislike him. But there were two other facts that clouded the horizon. The first was that my dear wife Dani had been the high school sweetheart of Fox Murphy. She claims it was a time of innocent, juvenile ignorance. I reserve judgment. The other problem was that Turtle's first wife, Mary Beth Haymaker, married Murphy two months after her divorce from Turtle.

"What are we going to do?", Dani asked.

"First, we're not going to go over there and kill or beat up anybody", I said. "Do you understand that, Turtle?"

"Yeah, but I don't like it."

"Second, I think we need to go see the Judge. Cagle's is in Cherohowla County and he'll sit on any case that considered it if we take it to court."

"Is that what we're going to do, take it to court?" Dani questioned.

"Jack, Haymaker's not gonna go against his own daughter", Turtle protested.

"Okay, okay, one at a time. I don't know if we'll go to court or not, but we still need to talk to the Judge. And Turtle, don't worry about the Judge's family feelings. He'll do the right thing."

"Yeah right", Turtle said, not believing me.

"Hey, he kicked you out didn't he?", I laughed, hitting Turtle on the back and making him swallow the mouthful of Copenhagen he was working around in his mouth. Any normal person would retch – Turtle just asked for a cup of coffee.

I called the Judge as he was leaving his house and he agreed to see us in his office on the square in Rosemary.

"Jack, Dani, Turtle – it's good to see you. Haven't seen you in church lately, Turtle. You know you don't have to wait – the door's always open". The Judge knew how to work a crowd and, even better, how to disarm potential troublemakers.

Turtle ignored the question and the invitation.

"How's the fishing?" the Judge asked, appearing to direct his question to Turtle.

"Judge, we didn't come here to talk about fishing," I interrupted.

"Okay," he said as he sat down and motioned for us to sit in the three chairs arrayed in front of his desk. "I expect you're here to talk about my son-in-law and Cagle's Knob. Am I correct?"

"Yes sir, you are."

"You're damn right we are", Turtle swore.

"Eugene, I will not have cussing in my courtroom and I will not have it in my office", the Judge reprimanded.

I jumped in again to save Turtle.

"We want to know what you know about this thing,"

"Unfortunately I only know what you know. Edward's not told me what he plans and I didn't have a clue Edward was interested in the Knob until yesterday when the newspaperman called me. I tried to call Edward and Mary Beth last night, but no one answered. I will tell you that I am as concerned with the fate of Cagle's Knob as you are."

At that moment, the door to the Judge's office opened and in walked Mary Beth, followed by Edward "Fox" Murphy. Turtle glowered. I whispered to him to stay quiet.

They were a pair. Mary Beth had been a beautiful girl in high school. She was still beautiful, but too much of her beauty these days was paid for. The visits to a Nashville plastic surgeon had blessed her with parts of her body that entered the room long before other parts did. It blended in well with the too-tight clothes she wore and the tanning bed skin and slicked back hair and tailored clothes of her ne'er do-well husband. Fox Murphy was destined from birth to be a lounge singer or a land pillager – probably chose raping land because he couldn't sing. I'd say he looked like a used car salesman, but I know good folks who sell used cars.

"Hello Daddy," Mary Beth gushed as she sashayed in, looking like Scarlett O'Hara, played by Dolly Parton.

"Good Morning Judge" Fox immediately followed and then, seeing the three of us, stopped.

"Well Dani dear - it's been too long since we've seen each

other! And Jack! And Eugene!", Murphy was pouring on the charm like a politician at a senior's center.

"Murphy you call me Eugene again and the Judge'll have to have me arrested!", Turtle said low, with the sound rumbling from his throat and the veins standing in bunched cords along his neck.

"Now, now, lets all sit down and talk," the Judge stepped in, seeking to avoid World War III.

"I apologize – I only meant to recognize you. What would you like for me to call you?", Murphy asked, somewhat confused, somewhat wary, and pretty much filled with arrogance.

"Don't. If I want you, I'll call you," came Turtle's reply. I could count his heartbeat by watching his neck veins bounce.

The Judge again became mediator.

"Edward, our friend Mr. Wallace prefers to be called Turtle."

"Oh, yes...I had forgotten. Turtle Wallace – the fastest running back in state history and the second fastest man to step out of Cherohowla County. A great twist on names – confuse speed with a turtle....very clever," Murphy seemed actually to be amused. "I do remember your speed years ago when you sent me and my teammates home severely disappointed."

"Tell me Turtle, tell me are you still fast?"

Turtle didn't say a word. He stared at Murphy.

Murphy blanched. The Judge arranged his seat between the two of them.

For two hours we talked. Murphy explained that he had taken an option on the land on and around Cagle's Knob and was planning an extensive development. When asked about the eagles that wintered over there on odd years, he had a plan. When asked about the old timber, he had a plan - and a carrot for Turtle, who was a lumber man. Turtle declined the bribe. When asked about traffic he explained the four-lane highway the state transportation folks and the Governor had committed to. But when asked about the brook trout that lived high on the flanks of the mountain above the falls, he claimed ignorance. As he did when Turtle explained about the bobcat and the black bear.

"Well of course we will make allowances for this sort of thing! My company is committed to green causes! We will make sure the natural ecosystem is protected and meets the requirements of state law!"

"Yes... you will, Edward", the Judge said resolutely.

We lived that summer in fear. Fear of what was planned for our world. Letters to the Governor, letters to representatives, letters to newspapers (save the Rosemary rag) had no affect – just the same tired rhetoric. Murphy had greased the necessary palms and had greased them well. The only thing good that happened that summer was, in a sense, a good negative – we discovered that the Judge disliked Murphy more than we did. Our hatred was philosophical. The Judge had a Fox in his house and he couldn't do anything about it for fear of wounding his daughter. And if he did try to stop it, some judge up the line would overturn his action.

Public hearings were held by the transportation folks – hearings where negative statements were politely listened to and all positive statements were recorded in the minutes of the meeting. I've lived in Cherohowla off and on for most of my life, with the exception of college, the Army and those confused years in big cities elsewhere. I thought I knew everyone here, but there sure were a lot of folks pretending to be homefolk, who drove cars with out-of-county license plates. Just like when the hearings for the Little Tennessee were going on in the '70's. Import supporters and suppress the local objections.

By October, we realized we were losing the battle. The only way to solve the problem was to hope that Murphy wouldn't raise enough money to pay for the options he had taken on the land. And that didn't look good either. Presales were reportedly going like hotcakes in a lumber camp. That's when Turtle had his vision, his inspiration.

It came after a week of fasting and living by himself on the peak of Cagle's Knob, drinking spring water and eating nothing but Vienna Sausages. Turtle later claimed his inspiration came from above. I think it came from eating six days worth of Vienna Sausages – Jerry and the boys with the Grateful Dead never saw such sights.

Turtle was ingenious. Turtle was inspired. And Turtle was committed: to the salvation of Cagle's Knob and the damnation of Fox Murphy. The fact that Murphy was one of the most dedicated striper fishermen in this area was all the information Turtle needed.

Murphy's company sponsored an annual striper tournament on the big TVA lake that is west of our county (we'll be anonymous here to protect the guilty). Stripers, as we know them around here, are actually hybrids – the mules of the bass family. You take a white bass and a striped bass and you end up with a sterile foraging monster that bends poles and snaps wrists with a fury that makes addicts out of those who fish for them. Stripers are relentless predators and love to eat baby bass and any trout they can find.

Turtle called in his chits that day. The Judge was on hand to be a witness. All the contestants – clients of Murphy Properties from Atlanta, Charlotte, Greenville, Raleigh, Asheville, and so on – folks with money and not a lot of patience – folks that got what they wanted and didn't want to be bothered – all the contestants were in their boats with their celebrity hosts. Included were the three bankers who had agreed to bankroll the Cagle's development.

It looked like the Judge and the Sheriff and the Game Wardens had all come to wish the fishermen well. That is until the head Warden asked to inspect the live wells of each boat.

As each live well was opened, the wardens documented the usual assortment of farm-raised rainbow trout that striper fishermen use for bait. And they also documented the smallish fish with wormlike markings on their backs and ivory-lined fins swimming amongst the rainbow trout. It does not take a game warden to tell the difference between rainbow trout and brook trout. The brook trout looked as uncomfortable in the plastic tanks as Murphy's face did the next day when his mug shot was plastered over the front page of every newspaper for two hundred miles. The clients were released, due to the largess and hospitality of the Judge Murphy, even though the newspapers listed their names as suspect poachers. Murphy was not so well treated.

The state folks don't care much for people who use southern strain brookies for bait. And when they find a fishy smelling gill net in the back of your LandCruiser and brook trout in your live well and mud on your boots that matches the mud on the banks of a certain stream on Cagle's Knob known for its southern strain brookies, well, let's just say that you are toast. When the personal lawsuits filed by your maligned clients are finished – well, you're not toast, you're past the point of being toaster crumbs.

Months later, sitting on the banks of a river in Eastern Kentucky, after having driven all day to chase two-year old trout in new country, I asked Turtle how he'd done it. He just smiled and laughed about the boots being the most difficult problem and how hard it is to get past the security system on a Land Rover. And then he sat silent for a minute and said a prayer for the brook trout that never got to see their lives played out in the waters of Cagle's Knob. And muttered something about how, sometimes, a few must suffer so more can prosper. Turtle the philosopher...

FLIES

"JACK, tell me somethin': you study psychology and philosophy while you were at college?", Turtle asked.

I looked at Turtle before answering. First, he already knew the answer. Secondly, most of the time when Eugene "Turtle" Wallace asks me a question, there is either a sarcastic dig coming or he is setting me up for an extended discourse on his own personal philosophy. Before we both had turned forty, it was me that philosophized. Turtle has always been a master at the cut-down, the sarcastic observation, the devilish commentary. Before his fortieth birthday, when given an opportunity to share his philosophy with the world, he mostly chose to grunt. Now as we see our fifty year marks coming quickly, it is Turtle that has turned into Marcus Aurelius – at least in frequency.

We were sitting on my front porch, drinking coffee, watching the morning mist lift from the creek that runs between my front yard and the road beyond it.

I answered Turtle's question: "Yes."

"Seems to me that a man can tell a lot about a man from the flies in his fly box."

This was going to be deep.

"Alright, oh great and wondrous philosopher of the ages, oh sage of Cherohowla, pray tell what great lessons do you have for us today?"

"I was over in Reliance the other day, fishin' the Bend and found a brand new box of flies, lyin' in that pool to the right of Little Rock."

He reached into his coat pocket and pulled out a brand new aluminum Wheatley box and handed it to me. It was a beautiful box, a full six inches long and half as wide. It opened to reveal thirty-two individual compartments, sixteen to a side, each covered with an aluminum-framed glass window. A piece of English art – the English who built this box would say it "al-u-min-ee-um", not "uh-loom-eh-num" as Americans do – they even spell it aluminium.

Each and every compartment was stuffed with flies. Dry Flies on the left, nymphs and wets on the right. There were the usual cast of characters – Adams, elk hair caddis, Cahills, and Hendricksons on the left with hares ears, pheasant tails, and princes on the right. But there were also Coachmans and Sparkle Duns, deer hair bugs and hoppers, soft hackles and no hackles, McGintys and zug bugs, and more. The box was pretty. The flies were ordered by size and identity. There were a lot of them.

"You wanna tell me how anybody can fish all them flies? Look at 'em – man, you'd spend half your time tryin' to pick out a fly if you had that many. That's the problem with fly fishin' today – too many folks complicate a simple thing! Folks need to go back and read that Yankee Art Flick's book. Then they might figure out that there ain't but a handful of flies they need to catch fish. I swear if I carried all them flies, I'd have a stroke from the stress of choosin'".

Turtle paused and spat, sending a stream of tobacco juice flying over Miss Dani's porch rail, splitting the free space between two of Miss Dani's rhododendrons. Eight thirty in the morning and he was already chewing.

"They's too many choices in this world! Like down at the grocery store – you go buy a gallon of milk and you gotta spend ten minutes decidin'. Do I buy whole? Do I buy skim? Do I buy 2% or 1%? Then you got to decide which brand! We need to go back to when there was kind of milk, period! How can you have 2% milk? What does that mean? What's the other 98%? Why would anyone want something other than all milk? It's like them flies in that box there. They're like milk - too many choices. Why? I bet I catch more fish than most anybody but I only fish three bugs."

"That is true, my friend. But then you always fish water you know. Remember when we went to Alaska and you argued with the guide and you didn't catch a thing. You still wouldn't have if you hadn't been jealous of me catching all the fish."

Turtle fishes three flies – Yallerhammers, Thunderheads, and a partridge winged and chenille tied streamer we all call Turtle bait. When the two of us went to Alaska, Turtle had insisted on fishing those same three flies. In a land where the trout live off salmon and not bugs, his offerings were ignored. After watching me catch fish one after the other, while he churned the river into a froth, he finally gave in and started fishing the egg and flesh patterns the guide offered.

"Yeah, well this ain't Alaska", Turtle snorted.

"You have a point. But my point is maybe this guy didn't know the water. Maybe this guy wanted to be prepared for any eventuality. Besides, how do we know it's a guy? Could be a woman."

"Yeah, women fly fish but no woman'd be crazy enough to walk around with a Wheatley box full of a Sears catalog of flies. Women are more particular – women ain't caught up in havin' one of everythin', except maybe jewelry. I'm guessin' that box is owned by a man. He drives a big SUV and he's definitely read too many books. Kind of like you."

"You know Eugene", I said, deciding I'd bait my friend with a verbal fly of my own, knowing that using his Christian name would do the trick. That's the great thing about friends – you know how to needle them when they get on their high horses. "You know that reading a book isn't bad for you. Look at you – you've read what, two or three books in your whole life - you're still alive. Maybe you ought to read another one."

"Pffft. I know I ain't the smartest guy in the world, but seems to me them books and magazines take the pleasure out a' fly fishin'. They tell you tie this, fish that, fish this way, don't fish it that a' way, yeah, yeah, yeah. A body got no time to fish if he's readin' all them books. And when he gets finished readin', then he ends up with a box like that 'n there. He ends up thinkin' you need forty different bugs in eight different sizes to catch a fish. I ain't met the man smart enough to remember that many flies or to remember where he put 'em. Look at you, Professor – you carry four fly boxes full of flies and you can't never make your mind up what to fish. And then you turn around and you're changin' your flies out for new ones."

He had me. I am an inveterate fly collector. I see a new fly and I tie up a handful and put them in one of the four boxes I carry in my over-loaded vest. This generally means that I have to remove flies in order to find room for the new ones. I go to the stream and I fish my newfound creation and, without fail, find myself going back to the tried and true variations that always catch fish. Then the new flies rest alongside their cousins, awaiting the day when they too will be discarded for a new fancy.

"The way I figure, you can tell a lot about a man, just by lookin' at his fly box. Take that box right there. First off, it's one of the big Wheatley's – cost 'm more'n a hundred dollars just for the box. So the fella's either got a good bank account, or he's got a big credit card bill. Now, look at all them flies. They are all tied well, no crappy ties in the lot, but he ain't the one that tied 'em."

"You can tell by lookin'. They're all tied too good. They're all tied to specifications. Most every tier I ever met was good at a handful of flies, but they weren't good at every single fly. There are always some flies that don't fit the design – either their ability don't hold or their imagination takes over and they put their own personality into the flies. You look at those flies and they're all perfect – but they've got no personality in them. No sir, I suspect they were all tied in some Asian factory somewhere by women who've never seen a fly rod, much less a trout. Women who know how to tie a #18 Adams, because that's what they tie day-in and day-out.

Ever wonder what those women think, over there tyin' these little bugs, not havin' an idea what the heck they're used for?"

It was a rhetorical question because Turtle only paused long enough to take a breath.

"No sir, the fella that owns that box couldn't tie a fly if his life depended on it. I'm bettin' he's a professional and he's got a big credit card bill. Ain't nobody gonna lay down that much cash for flies, so it had to be on a credit card."

"So you're a detective now?"

"No, not a detective, just a shrewd observer of the human condition. Take you for instance, Jack Macpherson. You carry those four boxes, most of which are full of flies tied by yourself, everyone of 'em lookin' like somethin' a cat clawed."

He was right – I am not a good fly tier. I do it out of a sense of obligation to the sport, not out of artistic love. The truth is, I do not like tying flies. But I do it because I believe I am obligated to. I confess that I tie flies because of peer pressure.

"Your problem, Jack, is that you are a fickle man. You are a promiscuous man."

"Hold on a minute. I've been married to the same woman for 25 years and I've not once strayed. You, on the other hand, have been through two wives and more girlfriends than Carter has liver pills".

"True, but the difference is obvious pal. I am a hound when it comes to women, but I am faithful to my flies. You don't see me havin' no flings with Serendipities or Madame X's or some Headlighted Yeller Sally! No sir, I am faithful to my flies. You, on the other hand, are loyal to one woman. But all that loyalty builds up and you explode in a fit of lust when it comes to flies. Jack, I've seen you fish fifteen flies in one mornin's fishin'. You go through more flies than a poultry farmer goes through dancers at a strip club in Atlanta."

"You see, every one of us chooses what he's faithful to. I'm faithful to my water here in Cherohowla. Yeah, we fished up there in the Big Country, but I'd rather stay right here. I'd rather fish my three little old flies and catch my little old Cherohowla specks. Now I might run around some, but I ain't traipsin' all over the country lookin' for trout when I got enough right here. You and the fella what owns this box of flies – Jack, you boys don't fool around on your women, but you want to travel all over, fish new water every day, and see how many new fly patterns the Umpqua boys are comin' out with this year."

I couldn't argue with him about me. I didn't know about the fella with the box, if it was a fella. But he was right about me. I have always wanted to know what was over the next hill. I was the one that always wanted to find that "new water" that I hadn't fished before.

A few days later, Turtle called and told me that the fella that had lost the box had called him. Turtle had left a note at the Hiwassee fly shop with his phone number in case the owner of the box came looking.

"Jack, come over to the house about dinner time. Fella what lost that English box is comin' to pick it up. I want you to be a witness that I was right about him and all."

So I did. Dinner being the mid-day meal, about two in the afternoon a nearly new Lexus SUV drove down the gravel drive to Turtle's house at the Creek Place. A well-dressed man and a beautiful woman got out of the vehicle. Turtle met them at their car.

"I'm so glad you found my fly box. I can't believe I left it. I didn't even notice until I was back in Atlanta. It must have fallen out of my vest," the man shook Turtle's hand.

"Yessir, that happens to the best of us I suppose."

We all visited for a while. Turtle offered them something to drink – they asked for bottled water. Turtle gave them water from the spring that feeds the creek. The man and the woman weren't sure about this, but once they tasted the water, they admitted it was good.

Turtle asked the man where he liked to fish. The man told Turtle about how he'd fished all over the country, that he loved the spring creeks of Pennsylvania and the high mountain lakes of Montana and the old, historic waters around Roscoe, New York. Before they left, Turtle asked them how long they'd been married.

"This November will be our thirtieth anniversary."

FREE-WILL

FLY FISHING, for many, is an opportunity to slow down and to reach into the past and to touch history. Sure, there are those who claim they choose fly fishing solely as a more efficient way to fish in certain circumstances, particularly to obnoxiously picky trout that seem to only have appetites for miniscule insects. The "lure" you must use in such cases is a fly, tied with thread, maybe a bit of fur or synthetic substitute, and perhaps a finely wrapped feather from genetically engineered roosters that are descended from fighting cocks.

The fly is so tiny, with bodies scarcely larger than the wire diameter of the hook shank, that fishing with a fly rod is the only real way to do it. Oh, some folk use a spinning rod and a bobber with the fly tied some distance on an un-weighted line below the bobber, but this is unwieldy and some consider it an abomination. Besides, the contraption makes such a loud splash when the rig hits the water that any respectable fish will likely flee to the farthest reaches of the pool. If you want to fish that way, I'll look the other way – after all, the only fish you'll likely catch are truly stupid and you'll be doing the entire genus of trout a favor by ridding its populace of such idiots. But it is an embarrassment: sort of like your Uncle Colston who still wears his '70's lime green leisure suit to funerals.

I understand that there will be some people who may read those words and pronounce me to be a snob. Such folk are generally easily recognized: they're the ones who ride around with those decals of a cartoon character whizzing on some car logo or some such thing. So be it. My friend Turtle's grandfather, the Major, taught Turtle and me early on that you are judged as much by the folks who dislike you as you are by the company you keep. It was the Major who taught us to fish with a fly rod and it was the Major who taught us to be men. The fly fishing instruction was easy; the being a man part was tough. It's not polite in some circles these days to use such phrases as "be a man." Some folk write it off as chauvinistic. Perhaps it is. I don't give a damn. Such folk should hang out with leisure suited Uncle Colston for a while and maybe they'd get over their sensitivity.

When I was fourteen years old, I went to live with Turtle. It was the third greatest blessing of my life, only surpassed by the birth of my children and the day my wife married me. It was near the end of the longest year of my life, 1964; a summer where I had buried my mother, whose heart had finally broken after my father had gone to jail one too many times. Turtle's father, the county sheriff, had personally escorted my father from the jail to the funeral service. After the service, my father went back to jail and the Sheriff took me into his house to live with him and his family at the Creek Place.

The Creek Place is still beautiful, but for a fourteen year old boy from a troubled family, who had lived his life moving from place to place, one step ahead of the bill collectors, it was magical, a place of endless surprises and life-changing peace. Turtle's family had settled there in the 1830's, shortly after General Jackson had sent the Cherokee to Oklahoma. Some of the local Cherokee didn't make the trip west – they avoided Jackson's soldiers by disappearing into the hidden hollows of the mountains. Later, some Cherokee married white folks. Most of us who were born in Cherohowla County have more than a bit of Cherokee in our blood lines.

Turtle's ancestors were shrewd in the land they chose to homestead. In choosing what was to later be named "the Creek Place", they picked acres and acres of Chestnut, Oak, Hickory and Poplar dominated wooded lands set interspersed with limestone ridges, beyond which rose the flanks of the southern end of the great Appalachian Mountains. Through it all, springs flowed up from the bedrock and created streams that became creeks, which became rivers that ultimately emptied into the Gulf of Mexico more than a thousand river miles to the south. And in those streams were cascades and still pools, filled with flashes of olive flanked fish with small red spots with blue halos and reddish orange and ivory bellies and white-tipped fins, fish that white men would call Brook Trout, but that were known to the Cherokee as *Unvjadv Ajadi* (oo-nuh-ja-duh ah-jah-dee). The brook trout have long since retreated further back into the mountains, following the example of the Cherokee, fleeing the invasion of red slashed silver tourists from the West and their somber brownish gold German cousins.

Three generations of Wallaces lived there in 1964, with Turtle's grandfather, the Major, reigning as Pater Familia over it all. The Major served with Pershing in The Great

War, the first Wallace to leave the United States since the clan had migrated to this country, from Scotland by way of Ireland. The Wallaces, like my people, the Macphersons, spent a few generations in Ireland before looking for more civil pastures in the New World, first settling around Lancaster, Pennsylvania and, then trekking southward to the land the Cherokee called Tan-e-see.

After the war, the Major asked for and received his discharge from Pershing while still in France. He spent a year touring the old homeland of Scotland, becoming the first man in Cherohowla County to learn the art of fly fishing. He returned to America and fished from New York to what was left of the Wild West, before finally returning home to the Creek Place. We never asked him why he had spent a year bumming around Scotland or why he'd played cowboy, but I suspect it was to find and touch something in his past and to soften the scars of the wounds of war.

So it was that I came to be taught that children fish with worm, bobber and pole and the masses chase fish with gaudy contraptions of blades and balsa and propellers or, heaven help us, plastic worms or kernels of field corn. But men of substance (the Major's words) fished with long rods and silken lines and feathered and furred flies. We were fourteen, Turtle and I, still children in the eyes of the law, but in the Major's world we were young men and we would fish like young men and he would teach us.

The writer Norman Maclean, another descendant of displaced Scots, wrote of being taught by his Presbyterian minister father that fly fishing was a Calvinistic regimen, performed to a four count rhythm.

The Major was not a Calvinist. The Major's curriculum was Baptist through and through with no room for ideas of pre-destination and firmly in the camp of Free-Will. The Major's syllabus was built on the concept of the individual finding his own rhythm.

The Major was a "mule" man, meaning that he loathed horses, which he said were among God's dumbest of animals, animals that would let a rider literally run it to death. The major believed the mule took the best of athletic ability of a horse, the endurance and judgment of a donkey and combined it with its own self-awareness. The result was an animal that could outrun any horse while having the sense to stop before it keeled over. The Major would expound on how a mule instinctively knew its own limitations, how no man could teach a mule how to run or how to plow or how to live, but that the mule was smart enough to figure this out for himself. And so it was that we learned to cast a fly rod. Later, both Turtle and I decided that part of the reason that a Mule was so much smarter than a horse was due to the fact that the Mule was never bothered with ideas about sex.

The Major was adamant that fly fishing was much more than knowing how to cast. He was the Professor Emeritus of Opportunity and taught us, his ready students, that dilettantes may worship flies riding high on hackled points in the film and that degenerate Englishmen may believe in the ritual of the Wet Fly, but that men of Free-Will understood that trout should be fed flies that worked. Thus Turtle and I were expected to become proficient in all three forms of fly fishing - dry, wet and that oft-maligned craft of nymph fishing.

I cannot say that we were good students of the Major. Turtle generally fishes three flies only, with the Yallarhammer being his first and most usual choice. The Yallarhammer is a cross between a wet fly and a nymph and is a fly born in the Southern Appalachians where it was invented by some hillbilly who, like the Major, decided that fishing with worms was for children.

The Yallarhammer has a yellow-furred nymphal body, likely originally tied with the urine-stained underbelly fur of a goat, with a progressive wrap of peacock herl. The tail is formed of feather barbs clipped from the wing feathers taken from a bird mountain folk call the Yallarhammer, more properly named a yellow flicker, a woodpecker of sorts. The fly is palmer hackled with a split wing from the flicker, with the end result being swept-back individual feather barbs that undulate while being stripped across a likely pool, or, if you saturate the fly with floatant (or, as we did as kids, with Vaseline), can be fished dead-drift as a dry emerger, floating in the film. Some folks claim the original was much simpler than this, with no underbody fur, or a very thin fur underbody, or with only a peacock body or, alternately, with a fur body and no peacock herl, but all agree on the palmered hackle. Personally, I believe the original fly could have been either way, for peacocks, while not native to America, certainly were not uncommon on farms, even in the South. Farmers, or maybe more appropriately, the wives of farmers, have always liked the beauty of peacocks. At any rate, there has not been a fish born in American fresh water south of Alaska that Turtle cannot catch with a Yallarhammer. I have watched him catch carp, bass, catfish, bream, trout, perch, walleye, crappie and even, once, a hellbender on a

Yallarhammer (and that doesn't include a certain beaver that Turtle snagged unknowingly). Once, on a trip to Wisconsin, he tagged three small musky with the fly.

As for me, while I fish the Yallarhammer, I am more of a Free-Willer, as instructed by the Major, but nowhere as accomplished or as skilled as the old soldier had been when he was alive. I'll fish whatever it takes, as long as it resembles a fly, to catch a fish. It's not because I'm smarter than Turtle, or that I took to the Major's instruction better than he did, but rather because I am cursed with bad luck when it comes to fishing. I figure I need every advantage I can use.

The Major died in 1967, two days after Turtle took a hand-off from Jerry Bob Whitestone and, behind the best block I ever made either in a game or in my imagination, ran for seventy-two yards to score the winning touchdown that brought the only state championship (not including livestock) Cherohowla High School has won. The Major had known that death was coming; a cancer had started in his prostate and had gone on from there. The stubbornness and pride that his ancestors had willed him kept him from allowing the doctors from using him for practice sessions in surgery. He had prepared us for his death by taking us fishing for a full week, loading us into his truck, the truck Turtle still drives, a 1953 GMC half ton, and driving us to the Little Tennessee River, well north of our county, to what was, in the Major's words, "the grandest trout river in the world."

He was not his old self on that trip. He could not walk far because of the pain and he slept in the bed of the truck while we slept in the tent, for at night the pain was the worst. But every day we fished and we caught trout. Oh what trout we caught: Tennessee brook trout that showed their patriotism with blue-haloed red spots and white-tipped fins. Big brown trout that the Major said fought with the same doggedness the Hun had fought in the Marne during the Great War. Rainbows, whorish in their bright red and pinkish side dressings, and who leaped, according to the Major, like the dancing girls the Major had seen in the Moulin Rouge after the Armistice. And every night, the Major told us stories and talked about life and told us what good men we would be when we grew up and how proud he was of both of us.

The fourth day, a Thursday, was the best day. He, the Major, was fishing a triple rig of wet flies, with what I seem to remember was led by a Leadwing Coachman, followed by an Alder, with a Yallarhammer trailer. He was fishing a wide pool that lay below a dairy farm. I still see that pool in my mind's eye, with the tall stone silo reaching to the sky, with the old man standing, casting, occasionally stripping and then letting the line swing and then more strips as the line straightened downstream.

On the Major's seventh cast, the Lord exercised His Own Free-Will and sent the Behemoth to dine on the Major's menu. The Major was in the midst of a tiny strip when the Behemoth hit. We watched the Major lift his rod and the bamboo shaft bent hard and the fish started to run, pulsing and pulling the rod downward, aided by the current, the huge fish straining to be free. The Major's arm muscles fought against the force, using what little energy he had left in his body.

The fish ran downstream and then upstream, with the

Major moving with it and keeping the line taut, stripping line when needed and giving line when called on. Seven times that fish came towards the major. Six times the Behemoth of the Little Tennessee turned away. But on the seventh turn, after the greatest battle ever fought between angler and trout, the Major slipped his net beneath the Behemoth and lifted to the sky a trout for the ages – a Brown Trout that, when laid next to the Major's rod, extended from the reel seat to a full dollar bill's length beyond the first guide – thirty-three inches of angry German trout soldier felled by the ancient Major.

The Little Tennessee was dammed by idiots and a fly fishing President in 1978 and with it died the Major's grand river. Occasionally, I will drive up to what is now a lake where bass fishing tournaments are held and drunks ride around on pontoon boats, oblivious to what was once the most beautiful river in the Southeast. I will stop the car and look out over the stilled water and see the silo that still stands. The silo juts up through the water like a water-founded missile silo, a sentinel over the now submerged pool where the Major took the last great fish of Tennessee. As I stand there, I remember the Major and how he made my life worth living and how he taught me the greatest lesson that I have yet learned.

"We all choose our own road."

For Brad

FAR AIN'T NECESSARILY FINE

THE GREAT LIE in classic fly fishing in moving water is that you need to be able to cast, as the old folks put it, "far and fine." For at least one hundred years, the myth of fly fishing is that any angler worth his or her wading boots must be able to, with accuracy and precision, cast seventy or more feet of line. Accuracy means you hit what you're aiming at. Precision means you can do it over and over again. So every day when the snow isn't falling in the northern climes and the rain thins in the southern climes, fly anglers quietly retreat in anguished surrender because they can't seem to be able to accurately repeat seventy-foot casts. The myth has a life of its own for the seventy-foot standard is applied to everything from three to nine weight rods.

Don't get me wrong, the ability to cast "far and fine" can be a great asset for the angler – after all, to be able to consistently (precision again) and with accuracy throw a five weight line seventy feet, or even sixty feet, requires a skill level that means the angler should also be able to throw half that distance and hit the target time and again. Many an angler will grow frustrated trying to cast the length of a tractor-trailer, when they'd be far better off to concentrate on practicing hitting a plate sized target at the front of their car while standing five feet behind the rear bumper.

I believe there are actually two different dynamics at work

with this idea of casting for distance. The first has to do with the testosterone that addles the minds of unsuspecting men. This dynamic transcends fly fishing. You can watch it in living color by simply showing up at your community softball field. Sit there for a game or three and watch the church league softball players trying to pull a softball over the left field fence only to have an uninterrupted string of long fly outs. Maybe even a better analogy is that other sport mastered by the Scots: golf, where thousands of weekend golfers approach the teed-up ball and swing hard with a 9 degree driver, attempting to be Jack Nicklaus, John Daly and Tiger Woods all rolled into one. In their attempt to drive the ball 350 yards, they only succeed in putting the ball 100 yards into the bordering trees to their right. Back when I played golf (a youthful indiscretion, which I hope the Good Lord will forgive), I occasionally played with a group of elderly men. Not one of them ever struck a ball more than 150 yards; but every drive, every stroke, was straight down the fairway. Me? I drove the ball 260 yards, but half of them were either hooked into the woods on the left or sliced into the bushes on the right.

The second dynamic is one that still to this day infects me: the idea that the good fish are always "over there", or in local parlance, "ov' yonder." "Yonder" is one of those words I try not to use in mixed company - that is with folks who are not, in Turtle's words, "part of our tribe." Years ago I was on a construction site in Columbus, Ohio, a stranger in a strange land, providing some bit of engineering to the local folk.

A fella at the site asked me where some particular thing was located. I replied "Over yonder".

The questioner looked at me as if I'd answered him in Latin and asked "Where the hell is 'yonder'?"

I replied in my best Southern Appalachian accent "Ov' 'air!" *[Translated: O'v 'air = Over there].*

A true English scholar will recognize the word "yonder" for its true roots in old English. The word first showed up in the English language around 900 years A.D. (or for the heathens out there – 900 years on our current calendar). Yonder was used for centuries by English Kings, Queens and Scholars. These days, it's associated with dumb southerners like me. My kids don't use the word. They laugh at my verbal idiosyncrasies.

If Maclean was haunted by waters, I am haunted by "yonder." I stand in rivers and find myself pulled towards what looks like more promising water, just a little bit further out, "over yonder." This "yonder" mentality causes me to either push casts too far or I end up moving before fully fishing out the pool in front of me, moving to what looks to me to be "greener grass," or more properly, "fishier water."

Although I can, if I hold my tongue right and with not much of a breeze, cast the obligatory seventy-feet with a fair degree of precise accuracy, pushing a cast that far doesn't do much on moving water. The problem is not with the casting, it's with the fishing – you can't mend line, you can't control line on the water when it's laid out over seventy feet with conflicting cross currents pulling your line one way and the fly the other. Trout aren't the smartest beings on earth, but they can recognize that a hooked bit of fur and feather being dragged is not a real insect. Thirty feet and in: that's where most trout are caught and that's where we all ought to concentrate our energies (excepting, of course, still and salt water anglers– sometimes, seventy foot or longer casting in still or salt water can be, if not a necessity, surely a comfortable luxury).

The "yonder" bug lured me away from home. First, it was to college where I learned just enough about Civil Engineering to be trained and where I met Dani. Then the "yonder" bug sent me to Uncle Sam and Southeast Asia and West Germany and Panama and more. After Dani married me and saved me from a lifetime of personal irresponsibility, "yonder" took me through a résumé full of jobs and different cities with each one supposedly better than the last. Dani endured my wanderlust. We had a heckuva time moving to new places, seeing new worlds, meeting new people, garnering more and more frequent flier miles which allowed us to travel to even more places. In fifteen years, we lived in seven cities, eight apartments and two houses, the houses coming when the first two of our three children were born.

But then one summer day, years ago, I received a phone call one night from my old friend, Eugene "Turtle" Wallace, telling me that our twentieth high school reunion was coming up and that I was expected to be there, or else. I didn't bother to ask what the "else" was – growing up in that part of the country took any doubts as to what "else" meant. Dani and I drove from the Hill Country near Austin, Texas, across the green piney woods of East Texas, across the Mississippi and the low rises of the state that shares that river's name to the greater undulations of Alabama, across the ridges of Georgia and then back to the green valleys and shrouded mountains of my boyhood.

The town of Rosemary, county seat for Cherohowla County, was not much changed from that of my boyhood. The Western Auto was closed: its building occupied by the state's Department of Family Services. But O'Dell's Drive-In was still open and the town square was still dominated on the north by the Courthouse, on the south by the Bank of Cherohowla, with the powers of government and commerce regulated by the Baptist Church on the east and the Methodist Church on the west. It's the same today, more than two decades later.

Turtle's dad was still sheriff. The oaks and hickories and poplars still grew tall on the hogback ridges and limestone cliffs, but there were far fewer dairies than I remembered and much of the old farm land was idle.

My second day back, Turtle took me fishing. I had not held a fly rod for a long time and it took me more than a little while to get the rhythm back. But my eyes knew to look for creases in the water and my heart told me there would be fish queued beside the runs and below the drops and ahead of the tail-outs. So I relearned how to cast the fly with the long rod, my mind forcing my muscles to do something they once did out of instinctive reflex. As the Good Lord would have it, I caught a fish, obviously not the smartest fish in the river, but a fish nonetheless: a fifteen-inch long rainbow trout with a bright red-pink slash down its side and with a scar across its back, just ahead of its dorsal fin, probably from caused by the claws of an osprey or king fisher or other bird. The trout had been smart enough to elude a bird, but not so smart as to refuse my poorly presented hare's ear nymph.

I fished a bit longer, in the same place, and then my eyes began to look for another pool. I saw a wonderful looking spot about fifty yards further across the river, where water spilled over a ledge in three separate plumes, cascading into a dark green pool. My eyes and imagination lit up and I started for this new promised land, this new water that certainly held the bigger, more sophisticated fish that would properly challenge me and reward my efforts.

I fell twice getting to that far-off pool. I fished for an hour and did not raise a bump, knick, or even see the slightest tinge of movement in the waters in front of me. I finally gave up with disgust and turned to wade to where I had entered the water.

I waded carefully back, taking care not to fall again, not to re-soak my already wet and cold self. As I came back to the original pool where I had caught the rainbow, a voice inside me said "Fish it, Jack...Fish it!" And I did...and I caught a beautiful eighteen-inch brown trout. I laughed and kicked myself for not fishing for such a long time and for living in places where these beautiful trout did not live.

Dani and I moved to Rosemary two summers later. I opened my own engineering firm. I still travel but Rosemary is home. I rekindled my brotherhood with Turtle and my wife finally got the old Victorian house she had always wanted. We have kids now and sometimes, I get the idea that I'd like to live out west and raise my kids in the shadow of the great Rocky Mountains where big cutthroat trout await my huge salmon-fly imitation offerings and where the kids can live in cowboy country. Sometimes the idea comes to me that I'd like to retire to Chile where monster brown trout wait for an Americano like me to coax them into dancing for just a while.

But when the sun rises over Cagle's Knob and I hear Turtle's truck tires crunching the creek-run gravel in my driveway and I see my daughter's face light up when her uncle Turtle sweeps into my living room with his Pioneer Seed hat pushed back and with his muscled arms outstretched, or when I take the morning coffee to my wife and we sit on the porch and listen to the mockingbirds singing their songs while the scent of honeysuckle and magnolia blossoms tinge the air, I am reminded that sometimes the water is not always better ov' yonder. Sometimes, the grass ain't greener and sometimes the fish are big enough where you are. Sometimes it's what you have that is the best.

Sometimes far is not fine.

DRAKES, AN OLD BROWN, AND THE TURTLE

EUGENE "TURTLE" WALLACE is, without argument, the finest wielder of the angle I know. I have watched him catch fish from pools where I have been skunked. I have watched him pull fish from waters that I thought as lifeless as the River Styx. But even the greatest of anglers has that one fish that is beyond his ability. And so it was with a certain brown trout that inhabited a deep hole on Connesewega Creek, which flows from Sharptop Mountain east of Rosemary.

We first heard the fish long before either of us saw it. We were camping beside the Connesewega on the third weekend of May six years ago, hoping to catch the Green Drake hatch – a hatch that, when it comes off, is a wonder to behold. Trout go stupid and anglers can have an absolute ball when they're not trying to keep the big bugs out of their eyes, nose and mouth.

Where we live, there are only a few streams that still have noticeable populations of Green Drakes (Ephemera guttulata). We suffer from two liabilities: acidic water and a preponderance of freestone creeks that don't hold silt for the burrowing nymphal forms.

Most of the streams flow over granite bedrock and the waters are simply too acidic to hold the Drakes. At least that's my theory. A few of our waters flow over limestone, a gift left behind by the shifting of tectonic plates half a billion years ago when the Southern Appalachians were shoved westward in a geologic cataclysm.

The Green Drake hatch is a fly angler's dream. The Drakes are big flies, not as big as the famous Montana salmon flies, but having a length of more than two inches, they are flies made for old men with failing eyes and trembling hands. They are porterhouse steak to trout that are used to mini-burgers. The fish go berserk as the nymphs rise to the surface and shed their protective husks. The Drake nymphs are burrowers and live their nymphal lives buried in mud. The mud comes from silt, fine sand, and organic matter that accumulates between boulders and below deadfalls and along the inside curves of streams where the waters flow slower, where eddies are formed, and the finer suspended solids in the water can drop to the stream floor. The nymphs rise in their great hatch, taking on their dun form, down here usually a week or so after Mother's Day. As you move north, the hatch is later and later – in Pennsylvania, for example, the hatch may happen after Memorial Day. In northern New York, it may be August.

We set up camp above the creek, with a stand of rhododendrons between us and the water. We arrived late in the day, just when we expected the Drakes to come off. After we set up the tent, we sat on the tailgate of Turtle's truck, me sipping from my flask, Turtle downing a can of beer, both of us enjoying the smells and feel of May. We were going to be there for five days. There was no hurry. When I was younger, I had to hit the water as soon as I could. Age has tempered me some – I take time to enjoy the surroundings more. Turtle is still working at it.

The water flowing over the rocks in the creek provided background noise; it was still too early and cool for crickets. The cicadas that come summer would drown out even the gurgling water, were still buried in the earth below, living their pre-adult lives as grubs, much as the Drake nymphs burrowed in the creek mud.

I don't remember who first heard the slurping noises that caused us both to take notice. It's hard to believe how that trout can slurp so loud that you can hear them over the sound of water spilling over rocks, but you can. We half-ran to the water to see the activity.

The water was sparsely covered with Drake Duns, some still struggling from their nymphal shucks, some starting to take flight. We watched as trout came up from the depths of the pool and holes opened in the water surface as the trout inhaled the big bugs, sucking the bugs and the water around the bugs into their mouths, the water rushing through their gills, the bug sucked down into the trout's gullet. The sight, even in the ever-dimming light of dusk, was so much entertainment that neither of us thought to rig up a rod and take advantage of the moment.

We moved upstream, stopping at every pool, to watch reenactments of the first scene occur over and over again until we came to the biggest pool. The pool stood above an old timbering ford. The pool was divided, in its middle, by a limestone outcrop that stood a good five feet above the water, stretching over 20 feet in width.

Standing on the bank at the tail of the pool, we watched a boil much larger than the others form on the right side of the downstream edge of the outcrop and heard a gulping noise that dwarfed the others. Turtle looked at me and murmured "Damn, that's a big fish!" Then he turned and ran back to the truck, his bulky frame disappearing in the gloaming.

I watched the fish feed for ten minutes before Turtle reappeared, winded, with his rod rigged and fly attached. He did not step into the water, choosing instead to stand in the old roadbed at the ford. He began to feed line out to get the distance needed to get above the rock. And when the distance was right, he let the line go and the fly arced forward, the fly disappearing into the darkness.

Turtle is an instinctive angler and his instincts worked. I watched him lift the rod and the line suddenly went taut, bending the rod. The fish ran upstream, above the rock outcrop. And then the line went slack.

"Dadgum, that was a good fish! DADGUM! That was a good fish!"

The next day, Turtle broke a rod on the fish trying to keep it from lining the rock. The fish played coy for the rest of the trip.

Over the next three years, Turtle hooked that fish at least twice a year, but he never was able to get the fish close enough to actually see it. Every time he hooked it, it would break him off or spit the fly.

It was spawning time and deer season and we had both bagged enough meat to tide us over, so we snuck off to do some grouse scouting...or at least that's what I told my wife. Sharptop has a resident population of grouse, scattered about hither and thither. I like grouse hunting. They erupt from the vegetation like feathered rockets. They are hard to get at and the hunter earns every bird he finds. None of that Minnesota flat country grousing. Here, a grouse hunter ends up the season with one leg shorter than the other and the expanded lung capacity of a pearl diver.

We parked at our May campsite and moseyed down to the stream. The leaves were still piled up in the eddies but the runs were clear. Here and there, I saw the shadows of fish idling in runs and the occasional flash of nymphing fish moving along the bottom of the creek.

I looked up and watched Turtle squatting and staring intently at the water in front of him. I exited the water and walked upstream to the next pool where he was.

"Got something?", I asked.

"Yeah. Look right out there," he answered, pointing. "My old friend, the May Brown, is out there and he ain't lookin' good".

I immediately saw the fish, but it took a few moments to notice what Turtle had seen. The brown would sit in the pocket water below the run, hugging the bottom, and then he would roll over and go slack. He would start to slide downstream and then would work himself back upright and return to his hold.

"He's been doin' that for a while now", Turtle said. "Only, it's takin' him a mite longer to straighten out ever time he flips up like that."

"Wonder what's that all about," I mused.

"Jack, I 'spect our friend's about had enough."

We watched the trout's dance for five or ten minutes...I'm not sure. Time seemed to slow to a trickle.

And then the big brown shot up stream like one of the mountain grouse exploding from a thicket, like it did every May when the first of the big drakes began to hatch. At the top of the run, the trout rolled over, went belly up and was no more. Turtle stepped into the stream, caught what had been the fish in his hands, and carried the fish to the leaf-strewn ground.

There were no signs of physical damage to the fish. The gills were bright, the skin untorn.

For a time, nothing was said. Then Turtle stood up, dusted his jeans off and muttered that he'd go get the shovel. And we buried the trout in the ground beside the ford's lower pool where Turtle had chased that old fish for years.

Who knows why that fish died? Maybe the rigors of fending off other males so he could spread his milt over a spawning red had worn him out or maybe he just got old.

"Death comes to us all, Jack. We all gotta die sometime. But damn, that was a good fish. Didn't he die fine?"

For Edward W. Laine who was there

THE GIFT OF THE TURTLE

IN 1997 I DIED. Cause: myocardial infarction. Symptoms: a slow burning sensation in my chest, beginning at the top of my stomach. Actually, it began more like a fluttering sensation, except it was much more than that.

Within minutes, it changed to a burning sensation that was followed by sharp pains that grew in intensity and frequency. Whatever it was, it certainly was not indigestion. Thinking it might be some sort of "anxiety" attack, I tried to calm myself. The problem was that I was already calm. I had been getting dressed on a Monday morning when the sensation began. Monday morning, 6am, the world was at peace with the early morning birds chirping outside the window of our bedroom. I'm a morning person anyway and, unlike most folks, I actually enjoy Mondays. Full of promise, full of anticipation, Mondays are the opening of the door into the week ahead. Not something to be afraid of or to loathe, rather Mondays to me are like a highway stretching into new country. Only this particular Monday was a highway leading to a place I didn't care to go.

Death - the great fear. By 9:50am, I was dead. No heart function, no breathing – in another time, they would have pulled the sheets over my head and gone out into the waiting room and announced in somber tones to my family that I was no more. But God worked His miracles that day as He always has and always will. On that May Monday morning in 1997, God chose the hands of doctors and nurses and the technology of the latter twentieth century to wrest my body from the claws of the Death Angel and give me another chance. Through the miracle of hundreds of joules of electricity passing through hand-held paddles and a stiff shot of adrenaline judiciously applied to that muscle we call the heart, God gave me life anew.

My wife drove me home two weeks later. I was helpless, sitting in the backseat of the car, clutching a heart-shaped pillow to my chest that sported a vertical scar as the evidence of the mechanical valve the doctors had replaced my old aortic valve with. After two weeks of Demerol and morphine supplied to my veins through catheters to deaden the pain and enough beta-blockers and blood thinners to fell a full-grown stallion, just riding in the back seat of a car was more sensory input than my body and mind could process. Spending two weeks moving at the pace of a crippled snail made any sort of speed mind-blowing.

So she drove slower and I gripped the pillow even harder. The drive from Atlanta, normally a two-hour drive, took four, as Dani dutifully followed my mandated twenty-five miles per hour speed limit.

Turtle was standing in the driveway when Dani parked the car. He started to give me a hard time about being lazy and making Dani drive all the way from Atlanta, but Dani stopped him.

"Hush, Eugene, and help me get him out of the car," Dani ordered.

Turtle reached in to help me out and I pulled away.

"Get out of my way. I'll get out of the car my own damned self", I fussed as I twisted to get my legs out of the door and to set my feet onto the ground. I was cranky.

"Well, I can tell you ain't lost your winnin' personality down there with those high-dollar doctors and their winsome nurses!"

"Winsome? Where in hell did you get that word?," I grunted as I tried to stand up.

"I read it on your tombstone. Give me your arm and I'll help you in the house".

"Read? For the love of Pete, what is this world coming too. Turtle reading? Think I'll just lay down here and die right now."

Three weeks went by. Three weeks of whining and griping and aching and missing the sound of water and the gentle plop of a rising fish. After three weeks of sitting around the house, trying to stay out of Dani's way, and failing miserably at it, I announced that I wanted to go fishing.

Immediately my wife said no. I said yes. She said no. I said "Stop me". She looked at Turtle for help.

"She's right, Jack: you need to sit here and rest up. Besides, I don't want to be responsible for you", Turtle said, between bites of Dani's roasted chicken. No more fried chicken in the house – Dani had listened too carefully to the doctors and was now dedicated to "healthy" cooking.

Healthy smealthy – it's a story as old as medicine – if it tastes good, feels good, or looks good, it's bad for you. My daddy used to say "I've known a lot more old drunks than old doctors" – that's the excuse he'd use whenever a doctor would tell him drinking was going to kill him.

"So you're in on it too?" I asked. Even Turtle was against me.

"Naw, I ain't in on nothin', Jack. You wanna go fishin'? I'll take you, but you're gonna sit on the grass. You can't wade worth shucks on a good day and I'm not gonna be responsible for your sorry ass fallin' and messin' up my fishin'."

"Jack, I really think you should wait", Dani said.

"I promise I'll be a good boy." I was begging. "I've been staring at walls for five weeks and I'm going stir-crazy."

I was ready before daybreak. Turtle was more sensible, and didn't show up until nine. I was as anxious as a groom before his wedding.

"What took you so long?," I demanded when he opened the door to the truck.

"Put a lid on it. You know as well as I do that there ain't no reason to get on the water early. Them fish will be there when we get there."

We went to the Creek Place. Turtle drove the truck across the pasture to the creek. Every bump and rut in the grassed field made me wince and hold my pillow hard to my chest.

"You okay?"

"Yeah, I'm fine … just a little tender."

"Look, you take it easy. I'm serious! You sit here and watch me fish. If I see you up millin' about, I'll load your sorry butt back up in the truck and take you home, you hear?"

"Yeah, I hear you. I promise to behave. Just shut up and help me out of the truck."

The scents of the grass, the trees and the water all combined to make a perfume that filled my nostrils and opened my eyes. When you've been away from something you love for a long time, it's not only your eyes that long for it, your mind longs for the scent, the texture, the emotional feel of a place. Scents are doorways to memories.

"You remember the first time we came out here together?" Turtle asked.

"What?", I asked, absent-mindedly. I was too busy staring at the water where it spilled through a short riffle and into the pool Turtle's granddad named "Daisy's Pool" for his wife.

Turtle was sitting on the tailgate, stringing up the old Granger.

"The first time we came out here together – you remember it?"

"Yeah, I remember."

"My daddy had locked your daddy up for peeing in front of

the Judge's mother when she was driving home from her ladies' club meeting. 'Course your daddy didn't know nothin' about it, seein' how he was drunk as a skunk and all."

"Thanks for reminding me."

The last thing I wanted to think about was the antics of the town drunk who happened to father me.

"Yep, I brought you home with me and you stayed until your granddaddy could drive down and fetch you. Stayed the whole weekend."

"I remember... I remember."

It was a wonderful place then, a place to escape, a place to hide, a place to explore, a place to be wild. Turtle's dad was the sheriff at the time and made a partial career out of locking my dad up, every arrest more than warranted. When my grandfather died, Turtle's grandfather and father took me home with them. I lived with Turtle's family until I left for college.

I learned with the Turtle how to cast a long rod with his grandfather as our teacher, his father as our coach, and his mother as the provider of wonderful wild cherry pies, or blackberry cobbler, or fried peach pies.

We were taught not so much in rigor, but to cast with ease.

"Don't bother with any notions of fancy style", Turtle's grandfather, the Major, would say. "Casting a fly rod is an athletic move that takes athletic grace. Hold the rod gently and go SLOW!"

We mostly learned by imitation – imitating the Major who was the master. He was the Fred Astaire of casting – never a wasted motion, never a wasted cast.

"No one has ever caught a fish with his line in the air," he'd say. "Put the fly on the water. Only fancy pant boys spend all that time false casting. Efficiency and moderation in all things, boys."

Neither of us ever really learned to follow those rules. I still false cast too much. Turtle has the efficiency down, but the moderation thing never caught hold.

And so I sat there and watched my friend limber his rod and cast, like the Major, efficiently: two false casts, just enough to get the line out, and then release. He stopped his forward stroke semi-hard and the line straightened and the fly began its descent. He twitched the rod with his wrist to put some slack in the line in order to limit the inevitable drag caused by the rushing water pulling the line downstream. The Yallerhammer settled softly into the surface film, slowly dropping into the water column. It was...a work of art.

And all things were right in the world. The pain of my breastbone stitching itself back together didn't seem so sharp. The ache of my back muscles seemed less dogged as I lay there and watched my friend doing the thing he loved more than life itself. And I rejoiced with every little brookie he caught that day and laughed at those that got away.

And when the day was done, and Turtle was back at the truck, he reached behind the seat and pulled out an old brass tube and handed it to me – his grandfather's Payne, a rod that I had dreamed of since the first time I saw it in the Major's hands.

"Jack, you know I've never been much on this love thing; never really understood what it was. But when you had that heart attack and Dani and me were sitting there in the waiting room, not knowing whether you were gonna make it or not, well...look...it ain't right to tell a man you love him, but you gotta know that I love you, man."

"Don't worry, Eugene. I know. But you don't need to give me the Major's rod."

"Yes, Jack, I do. He'd 'a wanted you to have it. Been meanin' to give it you for years and then, that day, in that damn hospital, I realized that outside of you and Dani, I got no one in the world. I want you to have it."

I didn't know what to say, so I said thanks and held the rod tube in my hand.

"Oh and one more thing, Jack."

"What?"

"You call me Eugene again, and doctor or no doctor, I'll whip your ass."

.

CULTURE

CULTURE MEANS DIFFERENT THINGS to different people. I have a cousin who lives in Manhattan but who, when she's down for a holiday, loves to drive to Gatlinburg and tour its "art" galleries. On the other hand, I have an aunt in Bulls Gap, Tennessee (population 759) who takes two weeks every summer and flies to Europe to tour the old cities, frequently ending up in Florence, Italy. She has a thing for the Medici. You never can tell.

Culture in Rosemary is typical of the small town South. It ranges from a small theatre group and ballet troupe to debates over which bass boat has the most reflective metal flake. Turtle and I are often discussed amongst certain circles (actually just one circle – the one populated by metal-flaked paint enamored worm chuckers that hang out at Jimmy Lee's Bait, Tire and Fillin' Station) as being somewhat elitist, purely on the grounds that we choose fly rods with which to fish. I can never tell if Turtle is flattered or angered by their snickers.

Just the other day Turtle found himself embroiled in a new kind of culture – at least for him. Turtle had made the singular error of agreeing to a request of my daughter before investigating what the request actually was. It went something like this. We were sitting on the front porch, enjoying the afternoon breeze:

"Uncle Turtle?," my daughter, the inimitable 14-year old princess who sleeps under my roof and depletes my checking account, asked in what appeared to be an absent minded manner.

"Unh huh", said the loquacious Eugene "Turtle" Wallace, the man who once won a debate in junior high school not by out-arguing his opponent but simply by staring so hard that the boy wet his pants and surrendered the stage.

"Would you do something for me, Uncle Turtle?", she asked with a voice so full of guile and deceit I was even taken in for a moment. Then I remembered who was using that voice, and I sat back and watched the Turtle rise to the delicate Ephemerella that had been laid out before his nose by my daughter-dear.

"Sweetheart you know I'd do anythin' in the world for you. Just name it and it's done", said the unsuspecting Turtle, not seeing the trap that had been laid.

SNAP! He was caught.

"I knew it! See Mama! I told you Uncle Turtle would come see me Saturday!", she exulted as she leaned over the chair and kissed Turtle's cheek, before skipping off to her bedroom and the telephone that sometimes appears as if it is growing out of her left ear.

"Come see her what?", Turtle asked, not asking the question of me or my wife Dani directly – the question was tossed out like a blanket, waiting to see who would grab the corner. I couldn't resist.

"My dear friend, you have by your own magnanimity signed on to attend Faire Lady Rebecca Macpherson's ballet performance this very Saturday." I said the words very, very slowly so that each word would be heard without interference – the interference of Turtle's brain working to find an excuse.

"Do not try to weasel your way out of this, Eugene," Dani said without looking up from the cross-stitch frame in her lap.

Turtle looked like a squirrel caught between two Feist dogs. I snickered and took another sip of the brown liquid in my glass and another puff of the cigar in my hand. It was going to be a glorious Saturday for sure.

Saturday noon rolled around soon enough and Turtle to his credit did not renege on his promise. To be sure, I never had any doubt in him – Turtle is anything if not true to his word. He drove up the graveled driveway, came to the side door, and knocked. I opened the door and gasped. Turtle was clad in a new suit and worse, a suit that actually fit.

"Lord, Dani: you better come quick. Gabriel's about to blow his horn. Turtle has a suit on!"

Turtle muttered something not nice as he shouldered past me into the kitchen.

"Well, I declare – Eugene Wallace aren't you a wonderful sight!", Dani proclaimed, smiling with feminine delight. "Mr. Wallace, you are truly handsome in that suit!"

Turtle is one of those folks whose shoulders are about

three times wider than his hips. He's the type where most suit coats would look like sheets hanging on him. This suit fit him like it a glove.

"Yes, Ma'am – I went down to Chattanooga Tuesday and met with this tailor down there. He fitted the suit to me. Got it in the Federal Express yesterday. Figured if I was goin' to the ballet with Miss Rebecca, I'd look the part."

About that time, the lovely and talented Ms. Rebecca came walking into the kitchen and promptly demonstrating her shock by dropping her jaw so quickly, you could almost hear the bones crack.

"Ohmigod! Ohmigod!", she shouted in that quick, excited high voice peculiar to girls her age, just before wincing when Dani reached out and pinched her ear, reproving her for taking the Lord's Name in vain.

"I'm sorry, Mamma – it's just that Uncle Turtle! You look so handsome! Wow!"

"I have come, Miss Rebecca, to escort you to the Theatre for your afternoon performance," Turtle announced in as formal a style of English as he could muster. And so they were off.

The afternoon performance, as my daughter danced the lead as Odette in the Rosemary Ballet's performance of Swan Lake, was as good a performance as their little troupe had ever done. Rebecca danced divinely with a smile that filled the theatre with radiance. Two standing ovations greeted the performers at the end, led with thunderous applause by one Turtle Wallace, who rushed the stage with twenty-four long stemmed yellow roses for our ballerina.

Outside the theatre, as the crowd started to thin, Turtle whispered to me that the evening Sulphur hatch at the Creek Place would be on in about two hours and if we hurried, we might just make it.

We rode in silence to his house and changed into more fitting clothes. I leave a set of work clothes at Turtle's house just for such things.

I did not dare bring up the afternoon's activity, waiting for his impression of the afternoon. He didn't say a word.

The Sulphurs took their time, only sporadically popping in the early evening. I caught a handful of smallish trout and moved down to the pool that Turtle was fishing, arriving just in time to see his rod bend with a good fish.

The Rainbow cleared the water four times. The fourth, and most spectacular jump, looked like a largemouth bass trying to spit a Rapala. The Rainbow came out of the water and seemed to hang for a minute with the late rays of the setting sun illuminating the streak of pinkish red on its flank, sparkling like diamonds. When it was done, Turtle flicked the fly from the fish's lip and sent it back to its watery home.

Later on Turtle's porch we sat and enjoyed our tobacco— me smoking my evening cigar and Turtle nursing his Marlboro.

"Turtle, that was one magnificent fish you caught back there", I said, the admiration clearly in my voice.

"Yep, it was magnificent, wasn't it."

The katy-dids sang their song in the dusk. A whippoorwill called.

"Jack, you know that ballet stuff ain't bad. I never been to a ballet. I can't say that I know anything about it, but I can say this – your daughter can dance better than any fish I ever seen. That's what I was thinkin' about when that fish came out of the water that fourth time. You know how time stands still sometimes? When that 'bow started doin' that tail-walk, all I could think about was Miss Rebecca twirlin' about on that stage."

"I believe they call that a pirouette, Turtle".

"Pirouette, huh? Mighty pretty word, pirouette. Brother, your daughter can out-pirouette any fish I ever seen. Maybe I need to go to more of them ballet things".

"You'd better be careful, friend. Pretty soon, you'll find yourself being a cultured man," I said half-smiling.

"Maybe so... Maybe so...

For Jess

CHRISTMAS

MY YOUNGEST SON, Zach, and I share a heavy burden: we both have birthdays during the week before Christmas. Zach was born on the 22nd of December. I was born on the 21st. I say it is a heavy burden because how does anyone compete with Jesus when it comes to birthdays?

Dani, my wife, and I have done our best to make sure that Zach doesn't get lost in the hub-bub of Christmas. It wasn't that way when I was a kid. Then it was always "Oh, here's your combination Birthday and Christmas present". I hate to admit it, but there were times when I was more than a little upset about being born four days before Jesus' day. That all changed after my mother died and daddy got himself locked up again and I moved in with the Turtle and his family...three days before my birthday and one week before Christmas.

The best birthday of my life, before my children were born, was that one. For in the confusion and anger and agony of having buried my mother just a month before and of the embarrassment of seeing my father taken off to jail yet again, I awoke on my birthday to see Turtle's father, his grandfather, and Turtle standing at the foot of my bed. I was fourteen years old.

"Well, are you going to sleep all morning or are you going to get out of bed and join us?" asked Turtle's grandfather,

Major Wallace.

"Huh? Join you where?" I replied, still half-asleep and unsure of it all.

"Son, this is your birthday and in this family, the men don't lay around all day on their birthdays," said the Major. "We spend the day where God intended men to be – in the field!"

"Get your butt out of that bed," ordered Turtle's dad, the Sheriff.

Turtle's mom had breakfast ready for us and I followed the lead of the men, hurriedly eating.

"Slow down, boys," Mrs. Wallace chided. "The day's not going anywhere".

"Of course, it is," replied Turtle's dad. "The boy was unlucky enough to be born on the shortest day of the year and we can't waste time burning daylight".

When we walked out the door, the early light of the horizon hidden sun was just starting to lighten the eastern sky.

The dogs were loaded into the wagon, the four beagles into the smaller boxes, with the two setters in the larger tandem box. The two men climbed into the cab of the 1953 GMC pickup that Turtle still drives. Turtle and I sat in the bed of the truck, shivering in the cold as Turtle's dad drove us to the first field of the morning.

We spent the morning following the beagles whose job it

was to flush rabbits. I shot twice with the Model 12 they loaned me. As I recall, I killed dirt. But the Major and Turtle each scored two. Turtle's father didn't shoot. As I think back on it, I think he had decided to forego hunting that morning so that he could watch me and make sure I didn't shoot a Wallace. I remember the Major handing me his rabbits to carry, telling me that one was for me.

As noon came, we skinned the rabbits and cooked them over a fire Turtle's dad had built. And then we went fishing. And it was wonderful.

We each caught "a limit", as I remember it. We were all meat fishermen back then. Catch and release was something the Sheriff did when the Judge was in a bad mood. It didn't apply to fish.

We ended the day chasing coveys of quail in the field behind Turtle's house. Supper was bobwhite quail with brook trout on the side.

Every birthday after that was a repeat, until college and the military took us away. When my wife and I moved back to Rosemary after spending the godforsaken years in the city, Turtle and I renewed the tradition, even though the Sheriff and the Major were fishing Heaven's River Jordan and hunting the Elysian Fields by then.

Two years ago, we again ate our morning's breakfast, albeit at the Rosemary Diner since my wife Dani is not a morning person. We hunted squirrels in the morning, following Turtle's little Feist through the woods. We ate roasted squirrel for lunch. And I listened to Turtle go into a hissy about how Christmas just wasn't Christmas anymore.

"Damn store keepers put their advertisements out before Halloween and all anyone wants to do is spend money, get presents, and run around like a bunch of blind monkeys."

I started to argue, but I really couldn't argue because I agreed with him. It really did seem that Christmas was lost to commercialism and fluff. Even the new preacher down at the church had preached the Sunday before about how Christmas wasn't about Santa Claus, but was about more serious things. We should be more reverent, he had cautioned.

Somehow, our mood never recovered. The afternoon fishing was slow...no: it was quite simply dead. Even Turtle failed to catch a fish. Me? I never even felt a bump.

The next day was Zach's 12th birthday. From the number of trucks and cars parked at our house, it appeared Dani and Zach had sent invitations to the half the county. The house was filled with Zach's friends. A few of the fathers had come and we all sat out on the porch enjoying an unusually warm day for this late in December. We talked about the usual things – the weather, the annual debate about whether the deer, the coyotes, or the newly arrived armadillos were going to take over civilization, and how the high school basketball team was doing. Then we began to gripe about Christmas.

Almost on key, Dani opened the door to tell us that it was time for the cake and the presents and we all went inside. The living room was stuffed with kids that I have known since they were born. They were all laughing and having a great time. Everyone sang Happy Birthday to Zach and I watched him rip into the presents like he was still six. I was a proud father as I watched him thank each of the gift givers and we all laughed when the occasional gag gift was opened.

After everyone else had gone home, we carried the trash out to Turtle's truck and I left with him to take it to the transfer station. We rode in silence for awhile and then Turtle spoke:

"You know, Jack, I am a complete dumb-ass: all this time I been gripin' about Christmas and how it's all about greed and the wrong stuff. And then at Zach's party, I saw what I'd missed. Christmas is a birthday party, Jack."

For Ty

THE SNAKE HANDLER

LIVING in Southern Appalachia and traveling as I do, I get kidded quite a bit about incest, moonshine, and snake-handling churches. The incest thing is not something any one in polite society talks about. I guess it happens, but not with anyone I know.

Moonshine is nothing to be ashamed of. In the old days, corn liquor (or moonshine) was the only cash crop most of the mountain folk could "get to market." A lot of medical bills were paid with moonshine. Sears Roebuck earned its sales in Appalachia through the cash generated by moonshine. Not a few doctors were paid for their setting of bones and dealing of medicines with shine. A lot of taxes were paid with moonshine money. And while preachers railed against the evils of corn liquor, few protested the coins from moonshine sales that were dropped in the offering plate.

Snake-handling is something else altogether. I'm not completely sure of its origins, but I believe it started in the 19th Century in Southern Appalachia when some itinerant preacher read the passage near the end of Mark's Epistle wherein the writer stated "And they shall take up snakes and not be harmed." The more ambitious also read "and they shall drink poison and not be made ill." I don't have any personal experience with the poison drinkers (excepting, of course, the moonshine drinkers, but the real poison folks drink arsenic and strychnine, or so I'm told). I have, on occasion, run into the snake handling believer. Say what you will about the sanity of it all, but you have to give those folks credit for a faith that's hard to find in our more rational churches. For the record, I am firm in my Faith in God and Christ, but I have never felt the need to test that Faith by handling snakes. Let me correct that statement: I HAD never felt the need to test my Faith, until Turtle showed me the need to do so.

It was a Wednesday and I was at the Feed store, picking up some dog food and mostly loafing. Feed stores are great places to loaf in small rural towns. The primary places to loaf for men are, in order, the barber shop, the hardware store, and the feed store. Each has its fans.

Barber shops tend to be dominated by political discussion, which by the rabid nature of politics limits my hanging out much at the barber shop. Too many old men who haven't worked in 20 years expound for hours on corrupt politicians and wasteful government spending and the evils of welfare.

The hardware store is mostly dominated by long-winded exhortations on the economy, of which the participants are greatly opinionated with their lack of real knowledge never an obstacle.

Our feed store is the gossip place. The feed store is where you learn about your neighbors. Sometimes, if you can sneak in without being noticed, you might hear something about yourself or your own family. Small towns are great places to raise children for many reasons, not the least of which is that you generally know what your kids are doing, or have done, before they get home. There are no secrets. It is a blessing and it is sometimes a curse.

I was at the feed store, listening to the latest gossip regarding something or somebody. I don't remember. Turtle walked in and was showered with the obligatory "hellos," "how's your mamma doing?" and "did you ever get that old John Deere running?" Turtle had bought a 1938 vintage John Deere tractor a few weeks before and had been tinkering with it – he had decided to be a tractor collector – gave him something to do when he wasn't fishing, poaching or piddling (piddling is half-hearted loafing or sitting around doing nothing, which is one thing Turtle has mastered).

Turtle pulled me aside and told me we needed to go for a ride. Going for a ride with Turtle generally means he has something to tell me that he does not wish to share with the good citizenry of wherever we are when he mentions the need for a ride. Our best adventures are planned in Turtle's truck, or sometimes on my front porch.

Turtle had discovered a new place to fish.

"Jack, do you remember Miss Brodaig?" Jack asked as the truck reached the town limits.

"Miss Brodaig the teacher? Of course, I remember her."

Miss Brodaig had been the science and math teacher at Rosemary High School when Turtle and I were students. Rosemary High is no longer, having been merged with the County High School. It's a shame really. Our class had graduated 42 students. Miss Brodaig was our teacher for every science, math and algebra class. Turtle, not the greatest student in the school, had excelled at the science, math and two algebra courses. It was English and history and the other social sciences that were his downfall. Turtle liked to solve problems. Memorization was not his forte. I remember when we were n the midst of the infernal classes on diagramming sentences that Turtle rebelled and didn't come to school for two weeks – played hooky for two solid weeks. If he had not been such a tremendous athlete, the principal would have expelled him. But since he was the athlete he was, Turtle won his reprieve by having to shovel coal at night for a month, restocking the coal bins for the school's furnace.

"Do you remember the farm she inherited from her uncle?"

"No. I don't think I do."

"Sure you do! It's over at that old place they used to call Cement, in the northeast corner of the county. You remember Cement."

"Wasn't Cement an old mining place?"

"Yep. It's a ghost town and has been for as long as I know. They used to mine limestone up there and then grind it and burn it to make cement back in the old days. It's just a bunch of old buildings now. I was up there last week."

"How'd you end up in Cement?"

"Was on a picnic with a fair-haired girl from up that way. It was her idea to have a dinner on the grounds at the old ghost town." He winked.

There was no sense in asking who the fair-haired girl was. He didn't offer to tell me and I did not ask. It is, I suppose, the unwritten rule of men not to ask such questions. It drives my wife, Dani, to frustration. I'll tell her of running into someone and she'll ask me how their family is, how their kids are doing or whatever. And unless they've told me in the course of conversation, my reply will be "I don't know. We didn't talk about it. I assume they're doing fine." Dani does not understand that men just don't ask personal questions. If the other person wants to tell us, fine. Otherwise, I can find out about them at the feed store.

Now knowing Turtle as long as I have, I know full well that he never tells me anything as personal as taking some fair-haired girl on a picnic without there being more to it than a picnic.

"So how was the picnic?" I had to ask.

"None of your damn bidness. But we ate our lunch at the quarry and you know me: anywhere there's water, I have to get a look-see."

"Unh huh."

"That quarry pit's filled with the most beautiful green-blue water you've ever seen and the springs that feed that pool must be somethin' fierce, 'cause there's a creek flowin' out of that pit that's as wide as this pickup is long. And that pit and that creek is full of csome dang big brook trout. It is a beautiful thing."

This was news.

"Did you fish it?," I asked.

"No. I was on a picnic with a fair-haired girl. I had other stuff to tend to. But I do know that Miss Brodaig inherited the whole lot from her uncle years ago. He never let anybody on that land and you remember how private the old teacher was. She never let anyone on it either."

Me: "So how'd the 'fair-haired girl' get access for you?"

Turtle: "She's a member of the church that owns the place now."

"A church owns it?"

"Yep, a church owns it. But Jack, it ain't just any church. It's a snake church."

"Come on, Turtle. You mean to tell me that Miss Brodaig sold that land to a snake-handling church?"

"No sir. She left the land to them when she died. I think old Brodaig was a snake-handler herself."

"Good grief. Well, that explains the privacy."

We rode on for a few minutes in silence, both of us pondering Miss Brodaig, old staid, quiet, hair-in-a-tight bun Miss Brodaig being a snake-handler, before I asked Turtle:

"So how do we go about fishing up there?"

"I've been studyin' on it, Jack, and I think I've got it figured out. My lady friend told me there was no way the preacher was going to allow no heathens to fish up there. And that's what you and I would be – heathens, because we ain't been sanctified by handlin' snakes."

"Turtle if that's what it takes, there are a lot of other places to fish. I don't mind snakes, but I don't plan on playing with them either."

I do not mind snakes. In fact, the fear that most people have in snakes puzzles me. I've lived my lifetime in the woods, jungles and other wild places. I've had first-hand experiences with three people to be bitten by snakes and not a one of them died. Most folks don't know anyone who's been bitten by a snake. Oh, they've heard stories of someone's cousin or best friend who was bitten, but they don't have any first-hand knowledge. Yet these same people will stand out in their front yard when there is thunder and lightning, just to see the show. And they all know people who've been struck by lightning. People are strange.

"Don't worry about anything, Jack. I got this snake thing all figured out. Give me a few days and I guarantee you'll we'll be fishing the Cement pit and stream."

I had to go to Tulsa for a project on Monday and was gone all week. When I arrived home late on Friday evening, after Dani had already gone to bed, there was a note on the kitchen island telling me Turtle wanted me to call him when I had the chance. It was late and I was tired so I put off calling Turtle until the next morning. When I did call him, he asked me if I was going to be in town the following Wednesday. I was.

"Okay. I'll pick you up at your house about four, Wednesday afternoon. We're going to go visiting the New

Jericho Overcoming All-Powerful Spirit-Led Church of the Pentecostal Redemption."

"What?"

"The snake handling church. That's their name," and the phone went silent as Turtle hung up.

Wednesday at four, I climbed into Turtle's truck, curious as a cat with a hanging ball of yarn as to what Turtle had up his sleeve. Turtle was smoking a cigarette and smiling like he had the world figured out. He has that sort of "tell" that he gets when he's come up with a plan for anything – he half smiles.

"Okay my friend, what does the great magician have in mind?" I asked.

"Sit tight and ride and all things will be shown in their time, Jack."

We rode for forty-five minutes on two-lane roads, taking our time, until we were just outside of what used to be Cement. Turtle turned down an old logging road and we both got out of the truck.

"Jack, you might want to stand over on that side of the truck. I gotta do somethin' here that you might get a bit squeamish about."

"What are you talking about?"

"Just stand over there and watch and do not bother me," Turtle said as he lifted the top off a plywood box that sat in the bed of the truck.

As he lifted the lid, I heard the rattle like dry leaves being rustled, like tiny peas being shifted within a plastic rattle. Oh good Lord, I thought. The idiot has a rattlesnake - which he did. It was fully five feet long, with a belly nearly as big around as my wrist. Turtle had a snake hook in his left hand, a long aluminum rod with a 90 degree hook at its furthest end, and in his right, he held a set of snake forceps, a odd looking thing with a pistol grip and trigger in his hand and metal jaws at the other end of the stick. He reached over the gunnel of the truck with his left arm extending to the snake hook and pinned the snake's upper quarter to the floor of the box. He then reached with his right hand and slipped the jaws of the snake forceps behind the snake's head and squeezed the trigger. The jaws closed on the snake's neck, about three inches behind its head. Turtle lifted the angry snake from the box and pointed the snake at me. I stayed on my side of the truck.

"Jack, get me that mason jar that's behind the seat on your side of the truck."

I retrieved a jar that had a piece of rubber stretched and secured across its mouth.

"Jack, what I need you to do is to hand me that jar. And then I need you to take the forceps and hold that snake until I can get a grip on it."

"You want me to do what?," I asked.

"Look: I'm going to milk this snake. I'm gonna hold it behind its head and I'm gonna force its mouth to open and I'm gonna force its fangs through that rubber and it's gonna drip whatever poison its got in its glands until we milk it all out. I caught this snake last Saturday and I've been milking it twice a day since then. What I aim to do will require this snake to be drained and I need you to help me."

I did not agree to help Turtle with the snake because I wanted to fish the Cement tract. I did not help Turtle because I wanted to witness a five-foot long timber rattler being milked of its poison into a mason jar. I helped Turtle because he is my friend and he asked me to.

I held the snake forceps with the trigger closed and the jaws tightened around the snake's neck. Turtle slid his right hand up the snake's neck from in front of the forceps. He grasped the snake immediately behind its jaws with his thumb behind the snake's left jaw, his fore finger on top of the snake's head, between the horned ridges above the snake's eyes and with his middle and ring fingers behind the snake's right jaw. He pushed down with his fore finger and the jaws opened with the two fangs popping out, curving back towards the bottom of its mouth.

Turtle took the mason jar and forced the fangs through the rubber and we watched drops of milky fluid drip into the jar. There wasn't much. Turtle had been milking it regularly. The snake was nearly dry of poison. Turtle just wanted to make sure it was as dry as it could be.

Ten minutes later, after putting the snake back into the box and smoking a calming cigarette apiece, we were in the truck, headed north to the New Jericho Overcoming All-Powerful Spirit-Led Church of the Pentecostal Redemption. As we came around the curve before the church, we saw several cars and trucks in the graveled parking lot with men in their shirt sleeves gathered in one group, women in long dresses with small children in another grouping, and kids of various ages playing in the grass beyond the parking lot. Turtle drove straight into the parking lot and parked beside the group of men, who turned towards the truck, curiosity showing on their faces.

A dark-haired man with longish hair and a sharp-beaked nose, wearing a white shirt and a pair of starched jeans was obviously the leader of the pack. He stood a step in front of the group and stared at Turtle and me. It was not an angry stare or a threatening stare, but it was not welcoming.

Turtle did not hesitate. He stuck his right hand out at the man and began talking.

"Brother, I take it you are the pastor here at the New Jericho church. Am I right?"

"You are. What might I do for you and your friend?"

"Well Brother, I have come on a social visit, a visit to say hello, to introduce myself and to make up for the years you've been here that I've not stopped by to say hi. You see, I came to realize y'all were back here when I met one of your church members." Turtle nodded toward the tall blonde woman who had stepped away from the group of women and who was half-way to the men by the time Turtle finished his opening remarks.

"I want you to know, Brother, that I too am a man of faith, a man of belief and a man who has received the anointing of the Holy Spirit."

The pastor never took his eye from Turtle, watching him carefully as if he was trying to make sure Turtle wasn't a crazy man. As far as I was concerned, Turtle was pretty close to being insane at that moment and what he did after the pastor questioned him sealed my opinion.

"You say you've been anointed but many claim to have been touched and filled by the Spirit but claims are words and words can be false promises. We here at New Jericho believe that God is a God of Action, a God of Doing, and is not merely a god of words."

"I recognize that Brother. That is why I figured I'd show you instead of just telling you. If you'd step back just for a second and let me slide over to the bed of my truck, I believe I can prove to you that I am what I say I am.

The pastor leaned towards the truck and saw the box in the bed of the truck, along with the snake forceps and snake hook. He recognized what might happen. He stepped back to see if it would happen. Turtle grasped the snake hook with his right hand and tipped the hinged lid up from the box, letting it fall open. The snake immediately started rattling, that same dry tiny peas in a rattle sound that I'd heard not a half-hour before.

Turtle was bolder now. He did not bother with the snake forceps. He slid the snake hook beneath the snake about a third of the way along its body from the head. He lifted the snake from the box with the hook, the snake hanging from the hook. He brought the snake across the truck gunwale, his elbow coming in to his side and the snake two and a half feet out from his right hand, with the bottom two-thirds of the snake falling away from the hook and the front third dipping down from the hook and then up as the snake raised its head to sense the large masses of heat of the people that surrounded it.

Turtle changed hands, holding the snake hook with his left and grasped the snake with his right hand, gripping the snake's neck with his hand directly behind the snake's head. He dropped the snake hook and lifted the snake's body so that it draped across his right arm. He then stared hard at the pastor and raised his right hand with the snake's head jutting from between his fingers and thumb. He held up his left arm and then released the snake's neck. The snake pulled back into a reverse "s" and Turtle waved his left arm. The snake struck out and I saw the long fangs sink into Turtle's arm. In less than a second, the snake had recoiled from the bite and was back into the reverse s-pattern that it had started in. Turtle's arm was bleeding from the two puncture wounds. He calmly laid the snake back in the box and tipped the lid closed.

The men and the women all gathered around as the pastor shook Turtle's hand. No one bothered to ask me if I had been anointed. I was more than prepared to confess I was just an unbiased observer. But I was not asked.

The pastor asked if Turtle could donate the snake to the church. Turtle had no problem with that and two men lifted the box from the truck bed and set it inside the pastor's van nearby. We were invited for dinner, but told them that we had to be on our way and we left.

Two days later, on Friday evening, Turtle and I fished the

old quarry pit and the stream that flowed from it. The fish were big, very big. The fish were not sophisticated. They had never been fished before. We caught several and released them all.

"My friend," I said to Turtle as we drove away from the quarry that Friday evening, "I have known folks that would do a lot of strange things to get their way in something but I never thought I'd know someone who would deliberately get snake bit just to go fishing."

"Jack, I'm pretty sure that pastor knew that snake wasn't carrying a full load. I 'spect he realized that I had milked that snake. The mason jar was sittin' there beside the box. He knew that snake was about as dangerous to me as a yeller jacket or wasp would be. But I figger he recognized that I knew what he was all about too and that I was being honest in my dishonesty. I didn't pretend. I had all the evidence there for him to see. Yet he showed himself to be a reasonable man. I 'spect his congregation appreciated us meeting them at least part of the way."

I do not believe that God intended believers to take up snakes to show their faith in God's healing powers. I know there are people who will go to extraordinary measures to get what they want. I have one of those as my friend, Turtle. Heaven help us.

THE TORNADO

A TORNADO CAME to my county one May Saturday. It ripped and it clawed and it blasted away things that weren't tied down. The tornado destroyed four mobile homes and one rickety barn. No one died, but a young lady who had lived in one of the destroyed trailers had apparently had been taking a shower when the tornado hit. She was discovered walking amid the debris, completely naked and oblivious to her nakedness.

Turtle and I were inside the Rosemary Feed Store and Gossip Parlor - the latter, an unofficial but more descriptive title, listening to the conversation. The tornado was the topic of the day for obvious reasons. It was generally agreed that the tornado only destroyed structures that weren't tied down. The houses and barns that had solid foundations may have lost some shingles; a couple of houses had been damaged by felled trees but the houses and barns with good foundations were still standing.

We listened to the gossip for a while and then went outside to get away from the discussion which was increasingly about the naked woman walking amidst the debris. We sat in two of the rocking chairs beneath the tin-roofed canopy fronting the store. It was early May and the tulips were blooming. The dogwoods were in full flower. The lawn grasses were getting high enough that every man knew he had less than a few days until the grass would have to be cut. Turtle was sipping a short bottle of Red Rock Cola. I was working on my fourth or fifth cup of coffee of the morning.

A blue Toyota Landcruiser slowly drove south down Main Street, puttering well below the posted thirty-five miles per hour speed limit. The Landcruiser was the old kind, the FJ40 model that looked like an old Willys Jeep, the utility vehicle that predated all the newer, sleeker, more common and less capable Sports Utility Vehicles that are parked in driveways of women and men who never leave the paved streets and highways. The Landcruiser had been well-used. The paint was faded until it was chalky. Mud spattered the sides and there were several spots of obvious rust along the rocker panels. The top and doors were off the thing, which made it easier to see the driver.

The Landcruiser stopped in the street just south of us with its turning flasher on, waiting for a northward car to pass. When the car passed, the vehicle made a u-turn, followed by a perfect three-point parallel parking maneuver between Earl Jackson's old Ford pickup and Monty Brown's Harley Davidson. Turtle lit a cigarette. I took another sip of coffee and pondered whether it was too early to light a cigar. It wasn't. I did.

The driver was a woman with shoulder length blonde hair that fell from beneath a straw cowboy hat, the hat appearing to be well worn based on its bent and sweat-stained condition. She had on a white button down oxford shirt that was tucked into blue jeans that fit the way jeans should fit a woman. The top three buttons of her shirt were unbuttoned.

The white shirt went well with her tanned skin. Her jeans were starched and pressed and creased. She was tall for a woman, maybe five feet nine.

Her eyes were covered by aviator style sunglasses so that when she spoke, I could not tell to which of us she was speaking. The voice was pitched low and almost husky, a deep contralto that reminded me of Lauren Bacall in the heyday of real movies...or maybe Demi Moore for the more modern. Maybe she smoked. Or maybe she liked bourbon. Or maybe she simply had a husky voice.

"Good morning, gentlemen."

We both said good morning back to the lady, Turtle touching the brim of his ball cap, me touching the brim of my summer hat.

"I'm looking for a man named Turtle Wallace. Can you tell me where to find him?"

"Suppose we could, but that'd depend on what you want him for," Turtle answered. He took a drag off his cigarette, staring at the Landcruiser, being cool, not looking at the woman. I wasn't cool. I looked at her. She turned her head toward Turtle.

"I'm a researcher from the university in Knoxville. My professor suggested that Turtle Wallace could help me with my research. Can you point me to where I can find him?"

Turtle hesitated, staring off again into the distance, deliberately playing with the woman. He said:

"Most Saturdays like today you'll likely find him here at the Feed Store until about noon, 'less he's off fishin' or mowin' hay or doin' what it is that he, Wallace chooses to do. He mostly likes to piddle. You know what piddlin' is?"

"Yes I know what piddlin' is," the woman was frustrated and it showed in her voice. "Is he here today?"

"Yes ma'am, he is," I interrupted. Turtle looked at me and winked.

She moved past us to the front door and I interrupted her again:

"Miss, I suspect you'll be more successful looking for Mr. Wallace out here on the porch. I believe Mr. Wallace prefers it out here where there's less gossip."

She stopped. I heard a slight exhale and then I heard her turn. She walked back in front of us and smiled at both of us. It was a good sign. We had been yanking her chain and she didn't get put out over it; instead she smiled.

"You're pretty good. I should have known." She extended her hand towards me and said "You are obviously NOT Mr. Wallace. I'm Elisabeth Paine."

Turtle stood up as I did. I didn't know whether to be offended by her saying I was "obviously NOT Mr. Wallace" or to be flattered. I chose to respond.

"Ms. Paine," I said, "I apologize for not greeting you properly. I'm Jack Macpherson. The fella here with the baseball cap on his head is Mr. Wallace. We're normally more gracious to our visitors but when they show up and ask for someone by name, we get a little protective."

She shook my offered hand and then turned to shake Turtle's hand.

"You would be Turtle. My professor is John Turlock. He told me you might help me. He tells me you know more places to find native brook trout around here than anyone."

"I know your professor. Him and me walked a few miles around here. As to whether or not I'm goin' to help you depends on what you want."

"I hope we can come to an agreement. I need your help in identifying brook trout habitat and in helping me access it and study it. I'm willing to pay you for your time. I have some funding for my work and I certainly will compensate you for your efforts."

"Pay is good. We probably ought to wait until I see what you're looking for. Then we gotta figure out if we can work together."

"Mr. Wallace, I don't think working with each other is going to be a problem."

And that's how Elisabeth Paine came into Turtle Wallace's life. She came in a little soft, very direct and stole Turtle's heart.

Elisabeth Paine spent a couple of days with Turtle up on the headwaters of Cherohowla Creek, above Cane Falls. The days must have been productive for Ms. Paine announced that she had to return to the university to pick up some sampling equipment and personal things and that she would be moving to Rosemary for the time being. By the time she came back to Rosemary, my wife had decided she could stay at our house in the room above my workshop garage. I had no say in the matter. Turned out that my wife didn't either. Elisabeth politely declined the invitation, informing us that she had a camper trailer that she would be staying in at Turtle's, down at the Creek Place.

Turtle and I did not fish together much over the next year. He spent most of his time with Elisabeth Paine, walking up streams, helping her take and catalog and ship samples for her research into the stream ecosystems. They did join us for dinner most every Sunday. At first I thought Dani would enjoy the company of Elisabeth, especially since Elisabeth had a more worldly view of things, shall we say, than most of the folk around in and our county. They did get along well, but Dani was suspicious. She never said so, but I've known her too long not to know there was something about Elisabeth Paine that did not sit well with my wife.

One Saturday in early November, five months after Elisabeth Paine had first driven down Main Street in her Landcruiser, Turtle called me at the house and asked me if I'd could help him pick up something that Elisabeth had bought at a furniture store over in Henderson, North Carolina. He wanted to pick it up Monday. We'd leave Sunday, spend the night in a motel and be back Monday evening. Work was a little slow; I had no appointments on Monday, so I agreed to go.

He and Elisabeth came for dinner as usual the next day. After the kids went outside to play, Elisabeth told us that she had moved into Turtle's place, acting as if this was news we didn't know. Elisabeth Paine apparently did not know the first fact of life in Rosemary: there are no secrets. Shoot, everyone in town and half the county knew they had shacking up for two months. I suspect there were more than a few folks who knew about it before Turtle and Elisabeth decided to do it.

Turtle and I left after dinner, riding in my truck which is newer, more comfortable and not nearly as pretty as Turtle's '53 GMC, and drove across the mountains on US 64 through the tourist towns of Highlands and Cashiers, on to Brevard where we'd spend the night. It was a long and slow drive because of the two lane mountain road and I was in no hurry. But Turtle didn't talk much and I kept my mouth shut most of the way. It was only after we had cleared Cashiers that Turtle opened up.

"Well, she's redecorating the place."

"Yes. Women generally do that. I suspect that's one of the reasons God created Eve. He put Adam down here to tend the place but Adam was like you, Turtle: he spent too much time fishin' and piddlin' and probably didn't spend enough time tendin'," I said.

"So you're sayin' God created Eve to help us tend?"

"No. I'm sayin' God created Eve to make us tend, to make us responsible. I mean, sure, women have their own lives and their own purposes and all that stuff. And we couldn't exactly continue the race on our own, they surely help with that. But I sort of believe in a half-baked way that women were put on earth by the Creator to keep us men from being the irresponsible little boys that we are."

"You're probably right. She made me toss out about half the damn furniture in the house and she's fillin' it up with all sorts of stuff. Most of it is pretty good though. But then she ordered a new couch from a place in Hendersonville, a couch that cost more than two thousand damned dollars. I ain't had a couch at the Creek Place since I took it over. Mamma had one but I gave it to my cousin 'cause she'd always admired it. It was some antique Victorian thing that nobody wanted to sit on anyway. Never liked it and was glad to be rid of it. I was happy with my old recliner that you gave me but she's making me throw that out to accommodate these two wooden chairs and the damn two thousand dollar couch. Two thousand damn dollars..."

"Don't throw the recliner away. We'll put it in my workshop. As long as Dani doesn't think I'm going to sneak it back into her house, I'll be okay. I remember when Dani made me get rid of that chair. I loved that chair, but it had to go."

"It ought to be different for you and Dani. Y'all married. It's Dani's house just as much as it is yours. So I understand that Dani might not like that recliner. I don't agree with her but I was glad she didn't 'cause that meant that I got it and I liked it."

"Well buddy, it don't look like you have it anymore."

We talked some more but not about much, all the way into Brevard, where we checked into the motel east of downtown. We went to downtown Brevard and had a beer or three at the brewery there and ate dinner at a little restaurant around the corner from the brewery. It was a nice night out. We did not discuss Turtle's new roommate or the decorating desires of the women in our lives.

The next morning , we drove on to Hendersonville, picked up the sofa and drove the four hours back to Rosemary and to the Creek Place where I helped Turtle put the sofa in his ... ahem...their living room. Elisabeth was not there. She'd left a note saying that she had driven to Knoxville that morning and wouldn't be back until late in the day.

Their romance flamed brightly that fall. I only saw Turtle at Thanksgiving and Christmas. Ms. Elisabeth kept him busy I suppose.

Fall turned to Winter. Winter turned to Spring. And then it was May again and the tulips were blooming and the dogwoods were in full flower. The lawn grasses were getting high enough that every man knew he had less than a few days until the grass would have to be cut. And Turtle and I were sitting in the rocking chairs beneath the tin-roofed canopy fronting the Rosemary Feed Store and Gossip Parlor. Turtle was sipping a short bottle of Red Rock Cola. I was working on my fourth or fifth cup of coffee of the morning.

The gossip inside the store that morning was about Ms. Elisabeth Paine and how she had packed up her things and moved back to Knoxville. The rumor around town was that she had not bothered to tell Turtle face-to-face, but had left him a note. I didn't ask my friend what had happened. I made myself available to sit with him, smoke with him, and help keep the Comanches from coming over the ridge.

Some time later, Turtle saw me in town and invited Dani and I to a party. "I'd appreciate it if you and Dani would come. No kids though. Gonna be a sort of goin' away party for my former roommate who will not be there."

We were at the Creek Place by five, along with a few other couples, Turtle being the only single one amongst us. We all shared in the food that everyone brought, the food that we had set out on the long tables Turtle had arranged in the yard down by the creek. It was still cool, with summer's heat a few weeks away. Ronnie West had started a small fire in the fire-ring near the picnic area. Folks were scattered about in little groups, visiting, as we say down here. Then Judge Haymaker produced a mason jar of clear liquid and the men all started to gather around him. But Turtle asked the Judge to hold off on passing the jar and asked me and a couple of other men if we'd help him move something first.

He took us into his house and he asked us to help him carry the sofa outside, the sofa that Elisabeth had bought for Turtle's living room. We carried it to where Turtle led us, to the fire-ring and the fire that Ronnie West had built. We set that sofa across the fire and Turtle asked for the mason jar that Judge Haymaker had in his hand. Turtle opened the jar and poured the contents on the sofa. We watched the flames engulf the thing and we watched it all burn to ash. No one said a word.

A Tornado came to Rosemary one May Saturday.

SANTIAGO'S FISH

IT WAS A LONG DRIVE. Turtle's sole surviving uncle, Cletus Wallace, had invited us to his place on the White River in northern Arkansas. Cletus had spent his life at sea first in the Navy and then in the Merchant Marine, serving on board ships from World War II to Desert Storm, a four war veteran. Somehow this seafarer had ended up in the Ozarks. He'd written in his letter to Turtle that he wasn't getting any younger and he'd appreciate it if Turtle would visit before he went on to the great sea in the sky. I was invited as the chauffeur – mostly because I have a more reliable vehicle than Turtle's truck which sometimes can't be depended on much past the county line.

You know how sometimes you're driving and the conversation's going well and the next thing you know, you somewhere that you did not intend to go? That happened on I-55. Turtle was driving and I was navigating. Only I was a navigator in title only, since I wasn't paying a bit of attention to where we were or what we were doing. The next thing I knew, the sign said "Welcome to Missouri." Being men, we decided not to turn around but to hoof it across country. I sometimes think that the reason it took Moses 40 years to cross the desert is because once he realized he'd taken a wrong turn, he refused to retrace his steps. Either that, or it was because the women and children kept having to stop for bathroom breaks.

"Take a left", I said.

Two miles later, we drove into the town of Braggadocio in the county of Pemiscot. Pemiscot, as I learned later is an Indian word meaning "Liquid Mud" - have you ever noticed how the Indians seemed to get their place names right? On the other hand, the white men who named Braggadocio were a bit vague.

More miles and more missed turns in places like Pocahontas, Fender, and Hoxie, we finally found our road in Imboden. This was becoming a trip of poetic name places and an odyssey that would have made Homer proud. Only Turtle and I were the blind authors of this epic. We drove past Agnos, Shady Grove, Viola, Ruth, Cumi, and Gassville, finally turning in Cotter. It was a good thing too – Flippin and Yellville were just up the road and Turtle had just warned me that if I didn't stop reading town names, he was going to pull over and beat me with a tire iron.

When we finally pulled into the gravel driveway, a rotund, smiling man was standing in the door, his face freshly shaved with the obvious signs of razor burn on his neck.

"Well it's about g__d__ time you got here. Where in the hell have you been? I've been expecting you for three hours!"

"This damned fool had us all over Missouri and Arkansas", Turtle muttered.

"Missouri?", the old man wondered. "How in the hell did you end up in Missouri?"

I made an excuse about being excited about the trip and not paying attention, hoping the subject would change. It didn't.

I'll say this for Cletus – he didn't screw around about fishing. We'd barely stretched our legs and he was telling us to get our waders on and get in the river. We did not argue. The old man led us to a wood deck he'd built above the bluff and pointed out the river, giving us instructions on where the fish would be lying, calling our attention to a grass bed submerged off the river's near bank.

I fished upstream and Turtle took the lower stretch of our new beat. From time to time, Cletus would call from his deck, shouting instructions at Turtle. I was glad I was well upstream and out of the line of instruction. Turtle was not happy, but we were guests.

Obviously, we weren't good students, because two hours later, we retired, beaten and with only a few suspected bumps for our efforts.

The old man was a story-teller and a collector of more stuff than you could imagine. He had a ship's anchor as his mailbox post – he told us how he'd found it in Alaska and had hauled it all over the world before bringing it to Arkansas. Ship's bells hung from walls in every room. His fly tying room was an archive. Thirty-gallon plastic trash cans held scores of fly rods and fly rod tubes. There were more rods than I could count without unstacking and separating the piles of them that lay about. Boxes were stacked throughout the house with reels, line, flies, and the various gadgets and gee-gaws that are unique to fly fishing. A sheaf of greenheart rods stood precariously in a corner. Some of the rods would be, once assembled, as long as 18 feet, with wooden dowel ferrule plugs and silken wraps. I had the notion that a museum curator could spend a week in that place and never catalog it all.

He told us how he fished the streams of the Basque region of Spain, after the Spanish Civil War. We heard how he fished from the back of a gunboat in the Mekong back in the early days of Vietnam, long before Turtle and I took our journeys there. We stayed up late - him talking, us listening.

The next morning, we fished downstream from the house. Turtle, as he always does, caught the first fish. And another and another. I hooked a strong fish that I expected to be in the eighteen-inch class. But, when I brought it to hand, it was no more than twelve-inches. The fish on the White are stronger than their size suggests. The limestone-rich waters and the never-ending supplies of sowbugs are like steroids for them.

"You boys kick up some gravel and get some bugs moving in the water", Cletus shouted as he moved downstream.

I watched him as he stood, facing downstream, throwing slack-line casts, casting out and then pulling back on the rod tip when the line started to straighten so the line landed in a pile in front of him. The nymph he was fishing tumbled free of drag as the slack line meandered in the flowing water. To his front, a dead-fall hung across the river, its roots still clinging to the bank from which it had once stood and from where the river had eroded the soil until it could stand no more. He let the line move towards the dead-fall and I was sure that he would get hung up. And when he raised the rod and it bent double, I was sure he had done so. I was wrong.

The line arced to the right, past the dead-fall and into deeper water. The tip danced with the surge of a good fish. The old man held the rod butt close to his side and put the fish on the reel.

The fish ran upstream to within fifty feet of me and I saw the shadow of something incredibly large moving with purpose. It turned and the water bulged with it. The singing of the reel rang above the sound of the flowing water. Turtle moved to help his uncle.

"Don't touch that fish, boy! I may be old, but I don't need help landing a fish!"

The fight ran for an eternity. The old man would make up line and the fish would run again. He backed up onto the gravel shoreline and worked the fish into shallower water. The fish was surely too long for a trout. But it was a trout, a marvelously large brown trout. The fish would have none of this and bulled away, back towards the shelter of the dead-fall. The old man moved quickly from the gravel back to the water, changing the angle on the fish. It worked – the fish's head was turned. It was now simply a matter of time.

The Brown measured thirty-inches with a girth that would have supported more. The old man refused to let us help him, other than for the measuring. He gingerly cradled the fish and eased into deeper water, pointing its head upstream in the current, letting the oxygenated water fill the gills, before letting it slide down into the water column.

That night the old man told us about how he'd met Hemingway.

"It was 1950 or 1951 – I can't remember exactly, but I suppose Papa was still writing his book about Santiago and that great fish. My ship had put in at Gitmo and I hitched a ride to Cojimar. I didn't know if he'd be there, but I knew that he fished out of there with his friend, Fuentes. I went to a bar and sat there for two days, drinking too much and waiting. The second day a big guy comes in alone. I knew right away it was Hemingway. He was still muscular – his neck was like a bull's; you could see the muscles of his shoulders straining through his guyabera but he was carrying a little more around his middle. He looked old – he was only in his middle fifties at the time, but he looked much older. His beard was already white and he had a limp. I stared at him too long I guess, because he looked at me and asked 'What the hell are you looking at?'"

"I was like a school-girl only I was half-drunk. I muttered something about being in the Navy and how I liked his writing and that I had come over from Gitmo to meet him. He invited me to sit with him."

"He asked me about my ship and we talked about the war – the German war. Hemingway told me how he and Fuentes used to go out and try to find U-boats in the Florida Straits. I told him how I'd been in the Merchant Marine and we had tried not to find them. I asked about the fishing in Cuba and he invited me to go out with him the next morning. I couldn't go – I had to get back because my shore pass was over. He laughed and told the bar owner to see if he could get me a ride back to Gitmo."

"A year or two later, The Old Man and the Sea came out. I remember thinking how Santiago reminded me of Hemingway, worn down by time and life, but still looking for the big fish, still looking for something to conquer. I remember thinking that Hemingway's fish was like his life - he thought that he'd finally gotten his hands around it and then the sharks came and there wasn't anything left worth taking home. I've been around the world more times than most men. I've fought in four wars. And I think I know what Hemingway and Santiago were about."

"The thing is, you never get your hands around life. Life goes on with you or without you. The thing is you have to find your pleasure in the pursuit, in the chase. Because if you are only happy when you land something or you possess it, well that's when the sharks come and take away everything you've put your value in."

The weather turned cold and the fish took lock-jaw. We fished two more days and drove home to Cherohowla County. We talked about the old man's magnificent brownie and how we wished we could move the White River east a few hundred miles.

Two weeks later, Turtle came to the house to tell me the news that his Uncle had called the night before. There had been a fire. Uncle Cletus had gone to bed and awoke to the smell of smoke. He had managed to get out of the little house on the White River in time, but the house and all the collected stuff stacked inside it was no more, reduced to ash. Cletus had insurance.

I commented to Turtle that the insurance could never replace all the memories in the stuff Cletus had collected during his lifetime, memories that were all burned now.

Turtle replied "Jack, I said the same thing almost word for word to Cletus. And he answered me by saying "The memories are in my head, you fool. What burned wasn't my memories. What burned was merely just the evidence."

For James

TURTLE AND THE PREACHER

LIVING in a town like Rosemary, county seat of Cherohowla County, has its ups and downs. Rosemary is small enough that everybody pretty much knows your business - population 5800, not counting bird dogs, feral cats, and the occasional black bear stumbling down from Grassy Top Mountain just east of town. But it's big enough to have its own symphony or, I should say, chamber orchestra - an eleven piece ensemble, organized by Judge Haymaker. To say they are on par with some of the big city groups would be, in Turtle's words, lyin' like a coon dog in August. But on a warm July Sunday afternoon on the town square they sound just fine with me.

Turtle showed up at the house one Saturday evening, unannounced as always. Dani and I were sitting on the porch and watching the kids play volleyball in the front yard while we strung green beans fresh from the garden. I have always found peace in stringing beans – there is a rhythm and symmetry to it, taught to me by my long-departed grandmother who insisted that "idle hands were the devil's own." You take the bean and snap off the stem end, being careful to not snap it completely - just enough to break the skin and leave enough so that you can pull down one side and remove the stringy filament that runs the length of the bean. Then you snap the tail and pull up the other side, hence the term "stringing". After a while you get to where you can do it without looking. My grandfather called it "women's work" but I enjoy it. There are worse things to do on a late summer day than to sit outside on the porch, string beans, smoke a cigar and take an occasional snort of whisky and talk with my wife while the kids play in the yard and woods around the house.

Turtle came flying up the road, dust billowing out of the tire wells, reminding us again of the drought that never seemed to end. It hadn't rained in six weeks and everything was drooping, seeking some kind of moisture from the heavens, save Dani's garden which is watered from a spring that runs along our property. He stopped the truck and Zach, our youngest, ran from the volleyball game and jumped in Turtle's arms. Zach is eight, full of himself and one of those folks who never meets a stranger. I've always said that when he grows up, he'll either be an actor, a politician or a preacher – all three require the same skills – and Zach has them in spades. Turtle thinks Zach hung the moon. Zach thinks Turtle's the only adult that he's met that hasn't grown up yet. I agree.

When they got to the bottom of the porch steps Turtle set Zach down on the ground and told him to run along and play; that he had some talking to do with Dani and me. Zach wasn't thrilled about this but Dani shushed him and sent him back with the other two kids.

"Evening, Dani", Turtle said as he climbed the three steps up. Turtle can get downright formal when talking to my wife. "Hot day isn't it."

"Yes. I certainly hope that we get rain soon. Everything is drying up and dying. Can I get you something to drink, Eugene?"

"Yes ma'am. I'd love to have some of your ice tea if you have some and if it wouldn't be too much trouble."

"Of course, Eugene, have a seat here with Jack. I'll be back in a minute."

Dani stood up and swept the remains of bean strings from her lap. She went into the house and Turtle sat down in the rocker on the other side of me.

"Jack, I got somethin' to tell you and Dani but I don't exactly know how to do it. So when she comes back out, I'm just gonna dump it on you. "

I didn't press him, though my curiosity was certainly up. We watched the kids running around and we talked about how big they were getting until Dani came back out with a tall glass of iced tea for Turtle and two tea cake cookies. Nothing for me – Dani had put me on another of my (also known as her) diets. The only sweets I could get away with were those that I could sneak when I went to town. Of course, even then I had to be careful because the store clerk was likely to rat me out and then Dani would know what I had eaten before I got the truck out of the parking lot.

"Dani, Turtle's got something to tell us" I said, hoping against hope that he hadn't gone and fallen in love again.

"Dani, Jack: I have decided to change my ways and give up cussin' and hell-raisin' and loafin'"

I didn't say anything. Dani was quiet for about three seconds. Then she exploded:

"Eugene, I think that's wonderful. And what brought all this about?"

Dani's been trying to convert Turtle since we moved back to Rosemary from Atlanta in 1990. I've told her to leave him alone, but once she gets her mind set, the best thing to do is to just get out of the way.

"Well, you know that new preacher down at Rosemary Baptist?"

"Yes, we know him, Turtle. That's where we go to church", I answered.

"Oh, yeah, I forgot. Well me and him went fishin' the other day".

"You what?", I asked, thoroughly puzzled. I myself had asked our new preacher, well not exactly new, but six months is still new in Rosemary, if he wanted to go fishing. He had told me that he would like to, but he had to spend his time fishing for men, not fishes. I had put him down as one of your typical too-full-of-themselves preachers and had let it go.

"Yeah, I was down at the feed store 'bout three weeks ago. In came Preacher Hardy. Everybody hushed and just kind of watched him. Then he walked up to me, stuck out his hand and said 'You are Eugene Wallace. I'm John Hardy and I want you to take me fishing'. I couldn't say no, not there in front of those yahoos in the feed store. So I told him 'Sure,

Preacher. When you wanna go?' And he said 'How about tomorrow morning?' So I took him."

"Where?," I asked.

"Well, I picked him up at four-thirty – you ever known a preacher to get outta bed at four-thirty in the mornin'? I pull up in the driveway at the parsonage and he's standin' in the driveway, rod and bag in hand and dressed in overhauls."

"You sure you're talkin' about the same Preacher John Hardy that preaches at the Baptist Church?", I asked. Hardy had been, for the six months we'd known him, almost too formal and reserved. More than a few of the members of the Rosemary Baptist Church wondered if he wouldn't be more comfortable as an Episcopalian, one of God's truly frozen people.

"Yep, in overhauls! So he climbs in my old truck and we drive the three hours it takes to get us over the mountains and up on the Tuck. The whole way he don't say twenty words. I figure he's sleepin', but every time I look over at him, he's lookin' out the winder. I'm thinkin' that this man's weird. He don't ask for nothin' – just sits there sippin' coffee from a thermos he brought himself. And when we get to Dillsboro, he buys breakfast for the both of us. When's the last time you seen a preacher pay for anything?"

"Well we get on the river about nine. Preacher's gotta get his license and I gotta get more smokes. We park up at Bill Purdey's place and I ask the preacher if he wants to fish together or if he wants to fish alone. He says it's okay if we split up. So I leave him, only I don't really leave him. I walk downstream a bit and sit and watch him, where he can't see me. First, I watch him rig up his rod – one of those new plastic things, not my style, but you can tell he knows what he's doin'. I'm too far away to tell what kind of fly he was fishin', just then. Later he told me it was some soft hackle thing he'd tied himself. Man, that guy can cast and mend. His first two or three casts looked like it'd been awhile since he threw a rod, but then he caught his rhythm and he was tossin' line like a politician tossin' lies. I watched him catch three, all good fish, and then I said to myself 'Shoot, he's gonna be okay', and I went on and fished myself".

"That's great Eugene", Dani said, both of us waiting for the story to continue.

"So, at lunch time, I went back upstream and we met at Jones' ford. We ate and then I kind of leaned back like I like to and meant to take a nap. But the preacher looked at me and asked 'Eugene, do you have any corn with you?' Now, I figured, the truth had finally come out – the preacher was a corn slinger. So I told him no and that I didn't appreciate him insultin' me like that. He just laughed and said 'No, No, Eugene....I don't mean that kind of corn! I mean the kind you drink!' Man, you coulda picked me up and mopped the ground with me. I didn't know how to answer him! If I said "Yeah", he'd probably preach me a sermon. If I said "No", I'd be a liar and I ain't told a lie, except to my ex-wives, in a long time. So I decided to tell him the truth and I reached into my backpack and pulled out a bottle of that stuff that the McIntyres make up in Loudon County."

"What?" Dani asked, shocked.

"I know, but I ain't no liar, least not to anybody I ain't married to. So I pull out the bottle, the preacher takes it, shakes it, looks for bubbles, and then takes a long snort. I was ready for the Judgment Day, I tell you. Then he tells me that while he don't condone drinkin' to excess, he does believe a little bit ever now and then is good for the soul. I ain't never in my life heard no Baptist preacher say such about whiskey. Now them Primitives drink wine, but they don't mess with whiskey!"

"Turtle, you're kidding aren't you?", I asked.

"No I ain't kiddin'! The man drank McIntyre's mash like it was spring water! Then he asked me why I didn't go to church."

"So what'd you tell him?," Dani asked.

"I told him I ain't never had much use for preachers. I told him that I know my Bible pretty well and there ain't nowhere in there where it says I gotta go to church. Well, he told me that I was right, but that he'd certainly consider it a personal favor if I'd go to his church. So I told him I'd go. Then he said he wanted to fish some more. I sat there and watched him toss Light Cahills and he handled the cross-currents down there next to the football hole like nobody I ever saw, including you, Jack. He caught more fish in that hole than I ever have. Then at two, he asked if we could go back home. I said sure and we loaded up and started back. He even offered to buy gas."

"You don't say."

"I do say. On the way back, he asked a bunch of questions.

And when we got to the top of the gap at Standin' Indian, I stopped the truck and we talked for two hours about how I'd missed the mark and how I wanted to do better. So tomorrow afternoon, the preacher has agreed to baptize me down at the Creek Place. Told him I didn't want no dunkin' in no swimmin' pool or church baptistry, but that I wanted it to be in a stream where trout live. Figured if I was gonna die to earthly things, it ought to be in cold water. He agreed."

"So you're really going to do this thing?", I asked, unsure of the whole story I'd heard, happy for Turtle but puzzled by it all: a preacher who drinks and fishes and wears overalls and who pays his own way. Will wonders never cease?

"Jack, shut up.", Dani fussed. "Eugene, I think this is wonderful. We will be there."

"Oh yeah, I wouldn't miss it for the world" I said and winced when Dani elbowed me.

Sunday morning came with a light rain, soft and cool, not heavy, just enough to put down the dust and give the ground a shallow soaking. I sat outside on the front porch, coffee in hand, watching the sun break through the clouds in the eastern sky, individual rays streaking across the yellow gray sky like the glory of God Himself. It is times like these when I am reminded of how insignificant we all are, yet how important we can be when we focus on the right thing: like raising your kids, being there for a friend, pulling a thorn out of the foot of your Brittany when she's gone into the briars for you.

We loaded up for church with Dani doing her customary

swing through the house, yelling at the kids to get ready, sending me in to check on the boys, tying their ties, parceling out their offerings to go in their envelopes. I grimaced again when I saw the eye shadow on the lids of my 13-year-old daughter's eyes. We have a deal – she gets to wear makeup on Sunday mornings and for the occasional dance at the school. I hate it, but I deal with it. Little girls shouldn't be in such a rush to grow up. At least mine shouldn't be.

As we drove down the drive to the highway, Turtle's truck turned in. We stopped, Turtle parked the truck beside the drive and climbed into Dani's Suburban, sitting next to the 8 year old who hugged him.

"Ya'll don't mind if I ride with you, do you?", he asked.

"Of course not Eugene. You're welcome to ride with us to church any day", Dani replied happily. She was thrilled – I was still suspicious.

"Truth is I don't feel comfortable going down there by myself. This is a big day for me."

"Yes, Eugene it is" Dani answered.

"Uncle Turtle, are you going to get baptized today?" Zach asked him.

"Yes, son: I reckon I am."

"Mamma said you're going to be baptized down at the Creek Place."

"Yep, that's so."

"Won't the water be cold?"

"I reckon so."

We got to the church just as Sunday School was getting started. The kids went their way and Turtle went in with Dani and me to the Couples class. To this day, I wish I had taken a picture of the faces in that room when Eugene "Turtle" Wallace walked in with us. Jaws dropped, eyes widened, Jerry Holcomb spilled his coffee all over the hideous cream colored polyester suit he wore every Sunday in the summer. I had commented on it one day to Dani. She, of course, sided with Jerry, saying something to the effect that God didn't look on the outside of a man. She had punched me after I quipped,

"I know He doesn't look at Jerry's outsides, 'cause if He did, He might rethink that thing about us not being naked. That boy's taste is all in his stomach."

Sunday School went well, once everyone got over Turtle being there. Then the same scene took place again when we walked into the sanctuary for church. Most of the older women came over and hugged Turtle, calling him by his full Christian name, telling him how thrilled they were to see him, and hugging him some more. Most of the men stood back and wondered what the hell was going on.

The sermon was brief, as Hardy's always were. In honor of Turtle, he preached on Jesus' appearance on the beach to the disciples after His resurrection. You may not remember – it's where the boys couldn't catch any fish, and they see Jesus on the shore, and He tells them to cast again, and they catch exactly one hundred and fifty-three keepers. And then He feeds them fish He Himself had caught and roasted over an open fire. Hardy talked about how when Jesus started His ministry that He first went to two fishermen and then, as He ended His time on earth, He again went to fishermen.

The time for the invitation came and as the choir sang "Just As I Am", Turtle walked down the aisle. The choir stopped in mid-song ... astounded.

Brother Hardy spoke up: "Sisters and Brothers, it is my honor to present to you as a candidate for Baptism, based on his profession of faith, Eugene 'Turtle' Wallace."

The Amens started with three old men on the back left row. Hallelujahs started from the third row on the right, where the widow ladies sat. Pretty soon, the whole church was shouting "AMEN!!! HALLELUJAH!!! GLORY BE TO GOD!!!!"

Word got out that we were having a baptism that afternoon at the Creek Place and that the baptizee was Turtle. Judge Haymaker called Dani twice to make sure it was true and then announced that the Rosemary Symphony would play. The mayor called the house to make sure that he had heard right. Through it all, Turtle slept in the rocking chair on the front porch, ignoring the soaring heat and the flies.

We needed to get to the Creek Place early and help Turtle tidy up a bit, so we left at two and drove the eight miles to the Creek Place, hidden in a cove (holler in mountain parlance) in the shadow of Grassy Top Mountain. Creek

Place is the name given the secluded spot by Turtle's great-grandfather who recognized the unique beauty of the place and the abundance of the trout in its spring-fed creek.

The crowd started arriving at three thirty. By three forty-five, the pasture was full of cars, pickup trucks, and even a couple of horses. I don't know how you count large crowds, but there were a lot of people there. Methodists, Episcopalians, Presbyterians, Church of God, Primitives, they all turned out, all except for the Jehovah's Witnesses. The JWs don't socialize with us, I guess.

Judge Haymaker had the Rosemary Symphony arrayed in a semi-circle: three flutes, two clarinets, and one oboe up front, two trumpets, a baritone, and a French horn behind them, and off to the left, Bobby Ray Johnson with his drums and tympani.

Preacher Hardy had Bobby Ray get everybody's attention. Bobby Ray chose to do so by playing the drum solo to "Wipeout" until the Judge knocked him on his head with his baton. The Judge had Dani summon the crowd with her trumpet.

The baptism was a lovely scene. Hardy did the honors at the edge of the blue hole, a large pool with a small waterfall cascading into it on the backside, a pool that holds at least three very large trout. I know – Turtle feeds them and we've watched them rising to the fish pellets. At any rate, the symphony played a piece from Copland's Appalachian Spring and then, as the baptism took place, the whole lot of us sang "Shall We Gather At The River". As Turtle and the Preacher waded back to shore, the Judge had them play "Ode to Joy".

It was touching, actually.

Everybody moved to the picnic tables and grass. Kids chased each other and some men tossed horseshoes. The preacher, Turtle, and me moved on upstream to Katie's Hole, so named for Turtle's grandmother. We sat there, Turtle smoking a cigarette, me a cigar, and the Preacher chewing on a blade of grass. A small hatch of tiny Cahills (Stenonema Ithaca), beautiful pale yellow flies, started popping. The preacher mumbled something about what a beautiful thing it was to watch insects rise, spread and dry their wings, and then take off into the world, like the disciples spreading out to share the Good News and then he got up and walked away.

"Wonder what all that was about?" I asked.

"Don't know. You think I look any different?", Turtle replied.

"Different? No, you look like you always do", I answered.

"Just wondered. I feel kind of different."

"You do?"

"Yeah, I think I got a crawdad in my shorts", he winked as he took another drag off the Marlboro and looked up at the sky, just as the sun went behind a cloud and the wind picked up. "Looks like it might rain tonight."

About this time the preacher reappeared with this rod in hand, lined up, and what looked to be a #18 Light Cahill hooked into one of the snake guides.

"You mind?," he asked, looking at Turtle.

"Go head on."

We watched him limber up the rod, false casting until enough line was in the air to suit him. Then, as pretty as you please, he laid the line out in a tight, reverse "C" arc, the fly floating softly down and landing with gossamer wings on the water surface. The preacher mended line as the fly floated downward, working to keep the tell-tale signs of drag from rippling the surface. As the fly swept beyond a rock jutting up at the near side of the creek, we watched him raise the rod tip slightly and the rod bent, strumming with the sign of a good fish on.

"You got him, Preacher", Turtle yelled.

At that moment, at that very moment, I felt the hair on my head stand on end. I looked at Turtle and he looked like someone who had put his hand on one of those static electric generators you play with in junior high school. His hair was sticking out at right angles from his head.

My heart started racing and then I both heard and felt a massive boom. It knocked me to the ground and everything was dark.

When I opened my eyes, I saw Turtle lying there, staring at me.

"What the hell was that?," he asked.

"I don't know."

I rolled over and looked at where the preacher had standing and he was not there.

"Where's preacher?"

"He's fishing."

"No he ain't, Turtle."

We both jumped up. Now we could see the pool and the body of the preacher floating face down, floating amongst the bodies of fifteen or twenty stunned trout. We both ran to the pool and waded in, grabbing the preacher by the ankles and dragging him to shore. There was no pulse, no breathing, his right hand burned badly and his hair smoldering. We laid him out and Turtle performed artificial respiration while I screamed for help and started CPR with my joined hands on his breastbone.

Doc Jackson came running and took over for me. In a matter of minutes, the EMT's arrived in their new ambulance and Doc grabbed the paddles, yelling "Clear" and then pressed the button to send two hundred joules of electricity through Preacher's still form. The body arched and twitched. Doc checked for a pulse. A second jolt of three hundred and fifty joules was sent at the press of the button on the right paddle. Doc put the paddles down and put his stethoscope to Preacher's chest. He moved it up and back and then ordered the EMT's to put Preacher in the ambulance.

"He's going to be okay folks. Looks like he took a full bolt of lightning and he's going to be able to live to tell about it."

Some folks to this day claim that it was the Lord Himself that struck down the Preacher for having the audacity to baptize an incorrigible soul like Turtle. Me, I think it was just mid-summer heat lightning. I prefer to think that the Lord saved the Preacher. Think about it: you survive a couple of hundred thousand volts coursing through your body with only white hair, singed eyebrows and third degree burns on your right hand and arm – I'd say that's a miracle.

The gist of it all was that Turtle has cut down on his cussin' and he occasionally goes to church, but only on Sunday's when the new preacher's out of town.

Preacher Hardy? Well he retired from preaching at the ripe old age of forty-eight and moved to Wyoming where he works as a missionary on the Shoshone Indian reservation and sneaks off to fish in high mountain streams when no one is watching and the sky is cloudless.

And the fish? Well, oddly enough, by the time the Preacher was resuscitated and hauled off in the ambulance, the fish had all recovered, save two of the biggest who died and were eaten that evening by Turtle's pet raccoon.

Me? I'm still here in Rosemary, though I'm a bit more careful about watching the sky when I go fishing.

Turtle still swears it was the Lord getting even with a man who'd use a graphite rod on Sunday.

For Mark W.

THE COMPETITOR

I HELPED him unload his gear from the back of my Suburban. There was nothing particularly remarkable about his gear. He had nice enough stuff with nothing that screamed "Pretender" or "Wannabe." On the other hand, there was nothing that I saw that looked to be more than three or four years old, if one happened to be the type that noticed that sort of thing. I wasn't. It was only in retrospect that I can say that about his gear.

I had not met the Sport before. He was a client of a friend. The friend had asked me to take his client fishing. Said that the client loved to fly fish, something my friend did not do. I agreed as a favor. The favor was unselfish in the sense that I've reached the point where I like to watch others catch fish as much, if not more, than I like catching them myself. On the other hand, the favor was selfish, for my friend owns property on some of the nicest trout water in the Southeast, water that is not accessible to anyone except those that have the key. My friend has the key. He likes the water, but he's not a fisherman.

The Sport and I put on our waders, rigged up our rods and geared up, before walking down to the river. I suggested the Sport take the best water, the water that starts at a stand of dead hemlocks and then flows through a series of runs and riffles with deep holes interspersed in river and gravel worn slots and seams. Those slots and seams hold big trout and I knew that if the Sport fished it right, that he'd be a happy man at the end of the day.

I watched him for a few minutes and realized he knew what he was doing. So I left him there and wandered upstream beyond a bend in the river to begin fishing myself.

It was a good day. I caught fish on emergers and dries for three hours. Then, like magic, they stopped rising and I switched to a triple nymph and wet rig and began catching fish on the bottom. It was a remarkable day and I was happy.

Eventually, I wandered back to the car and sat on the grassed bank, smoking a cigar and enjoying a wee nip of the brown water I'd poured in the flask that morning, in hopes of such a time of rest as this. I watched a mallard family, with Father Drake and Mother Hen, leading a column of ducklings along the bank of the river. A Kingfisher flew by and lit on the Sassafras that over hung the river where the sawmill had once been, back when they logged the place in the '20's...the 1920's. I thought about the fish I'd caught and I smiled at the ducks and I breathed deeply, inhaling the clear air of the North Carolina mountains. I was a happy man.

The Sport hailed me and I looked to see him walking up the road, back towards me and the car. I stood up and met him, handing him the flask and offering him a nip. He tossed back the flask and emptied it. I secretly thanked myself for bringing the small flask.

I asked him how he had done. He replied "Caught thirty-one fish. See, right here on my counter, 31!"

I looked and damned if he did not have a tally counter hanging from his vest. It was a horrible looking thing, the kind you see at ticket gates where the attendant stands and counts the number of folks entering the place in order to keep the Fire Marshal happy. Bright chrome metal with a thumb ring, a reset button and a dial with four digits...I suppose for those really good days when he caught more than a thousand fish. It was all I could do to keep my mouth shut.

He went on to tell me he had caught six fish that were over fifteen inches long and he listed them, reading the numbers off of a pad he had pulled out of his chest pocket. He showed me the tape measure he had affixed to his net, as evidence that his eighteen-inch fish was truly an eighteen-inch fish.

He asked me how I had done. I replied that it had been a good day. He asked me how many I caught. I smiled and told him a few.

"More than twelve?", he asked.

"Probably", I replied.

"How many?"

"Don't know. I didn't count."

"Then how do you know how many you caught?", he asked, the impatience growing in his voice.

We loaded everything up in the Suburban and began the 3-hour drive home. The Sport thanked me several times for taking him. He repeated his wonder at how many fish he caught and how big they were. I was polite and I kept my big mouth shut.

Five days later, a small package came in the mail. Inside the package was a tally counter, just like the one the Sport had pinned to his vest. Along with the counter was a note from the Sport thanking me for the outing and explaining that he thought I might like a tally counter to pin on my vest.

I put the counter back in the box. And then I dropped the lot into the trash can beside my desk.

MEMORIAL DAY

ON A PARTICULAR MONDAY in May I go fishing. I travel alone and I fish alone and I am in contrast to most everyone else on that day that is spent, by most, with drink, barbeque, and outdoor fun. It is the unofficial first day of summer.

The rivers are crowded. My favorite streams are packed with corn chuckers, bait slingers, and hardware throwers. It is not the sort of peaceful fishing environment sought after by most fly fishermen. But the crowds don't know about Sweetwater Falls and the rhododendron-lined brook above it, tucked two miles back in Juniper Hollow and accessible only by feet that know the pathway and have the permission of the land holder. That permission would be hard to get these days. I buried him four years ago after the old wounds finally caught up with him. He left me trustee over a piece of timber covered land, old and green and gray and wrinkled.

Sweetwater Falls shows up readily enough on the USGS topographic map. The blue line crossing a set of crunched together contour lines is a dead give-away. The water drops eighty feet in three steps that serve not just to please the eye and ear, although that would be good enough. No, the falls have an even bigger affect – they are as a natural barrier from the imported rainbows and brown trout that the government started stocking in this part of the country more than a hundred years ago.

Salvenius fontinalis (southern strain) is still lord over Sweetwater Creek above the falls, sharing the water with only a smattering of mayfly nymphs and a sparse population of stoneflies, none longer than two centimeters on their best day. The insect population is large enough to support the brook trout but it is not large enough to allow the brook trout to attain any size to speak of. A brookie of ten inches is large. In thirty years of fishing Sweetwater, I've caught one twelve incher, released her and never saw her again. Most of the fish are in the six to eight-inch category and stay that way. I caught the same fish three years running out of what I call Juni's pool. A scar on its left side just beyond the anal fin was the identifier. For three years that fish never grew. *Salvenius fontinalis abbreviatus.*

So I awoke, another May Monday in another year and gently kissed my sleeping wife good-bye. I was careful not to wake her as I stole out the backdoor, pulling on my pants and boots once I was outside, on the porch. The sky was still dark and the birds were still asleep. I like to awake early on this day, partly because I like sunrises, partly because I like the smell of coffee perked on a camp stove in the woods before the sun warms the earth, but mostly because that's the way he would have done it and did do it for the twenty-six years we fished together on Mondays in Mays past.

The truck was packed the night before, just after I got home with the kids from church. I let it roll silently backward down the driveway and only started the engine when I was well away from the house and out of danger of waking anyone. I love my wife and kids dearly and love fishing with them and just spending time with them. But this day doesn't belong to them or, for that matter, me.

The drive was quiet and filled with sweet late spring night air. Above, the stars sparkled like a big city planetarium.

Occasionally, I drove past a dairy farm. Dairy used to be big business around here, but like a lot of things, the dairy farming business has seen better days. The smell of silage and cow manure wafted through the cab.

Finally, just as the eastern sky began to turn that grayish blue gray of predawn, I came to the graveled drive and stopped the truck. I got out and unlocked the gate and opened it. And then I drove the 300 yards into the hardwoods at the throat of Juniper Hollow, stopping near the burned stones that once were the foundation for the old man's home. I dropped the truck tailgate and winced when it slammed, metal ringing like a struck bell. I cursed myself for not catching it.

The single burner backpack stove fired up like it always does – pump like a demon, turn the crank, strike a match, open the valve, pump like a demon again, rotate the crank three times and then adjust the flame. I leaned back in the bed of the truck, watching the stars as the coffee pot warmed and then, after a few minutes, began to perk. The hissing of the stove and the soft slamming of water against the clear plastic perk top of the pot blended with the waking sounds of the earth as the birds answered with their song and a rooster crowed. *Probably from Lester's place down the road*, I thought. Lester raises fighting cocks and one of them is always crowing about something, or maybe just to hear himself crow. Roosters are a lot like people. Some strut and yap all the time. Those you ignore. The ones who walk slowly, proudly, but silently – those are the ones you bet on when the birds hit the floor. Least that what the old man taught me. I quit the cockfights long ago.

I watched a meteorite streak slowly across the sky, breaking into pieces just before it disappeared, low over the western ridge that frames the hollow on that side. Terribly low, I thought, as I poured my first cup of coffee of the day. Coffee in the woods, strong from the percolator and framed by the early morning air, is wonderful.

Mornings in the woods are what man was made for. God walked with Adam in the Garden in the morning. I like to think He taught Adam to fish in a stream like Sweetwater, with a long rod strung with a gossamer line and with an angel-haired fly, not unlike how the old man taught me when I came back, soul-scarred and tattered, from a hell covered in heat, humidity, blood, terror and black clad men who wished you out of their country and treacherous "friends" who changed shape before your eyes.

Finishing my coffee, I picked up the pack and rod and walked up the hollow and to the falls. If you climb to the top of the falls via the side trail the old man cut long ago, you save yourself the five hundred meter or so roundtrip to the bottom of the falls, but I always like to see where the falls empty. I hike to the base of the falls and pay homage to the water sprites that dance in the mists and froth of the tumbling waters. Sometimes I'll stand there and remember the night he baptized me in the plunge pool, washing away the blood and agony and self-doubt and listlessness that the year in the jungle had left me.

And so I did that morning, sitting again on the rock that I had sat on that night, when I had cried and screamed while he held me, letting the demons exorcise themselves after being purified by the cleansing waters of the old man's creek.

I lit up a cigarette, a Lucky Strike - his favorite - and coughed at the first rush of smoke to my lungs since the year before. I forced myself to inhale deeply each time until the weed was no more and then placed the cigarette pack, full save the one just smoked, in the hollow of the sassafras tree that stands on the east bank of the stream and at the tail of the plunge pool. Then I took the path to the top of the falls.

You fish this water stealthily, like an animal. It is not picture book fly fishing where the angler stands in the middle of a wide pool and casts a rod back and forth in tight arcs, slinging a fly 60 feet away. You can't see 60 feet in some places, much less cast. The water is so clear and the trout so wary, that just stepping into the water will give lockjaw to every trout between there and the next county. No, on Sweetwater you get down on your knees and crawl forward through the rhododendron and extend your rod over the pool, letting the #16 anything dap the surface of the water. I say #16 anything because that is the way it is. The old man taught me that these trout were too hungry and food too damn scarce to be picky in what they ate. Put out anything resembling a bug in a size #16 and they will grab it.

From the first pool, I caught two beautiful fish, deep olive flanks spotted with blue-haloed red specks and reddish amber bronze bellies and worm trails tattooed on their upper sides. Second pool, same results. Third pool, Juni's pool, no fish, no sign of a fish, no shadows, no streaks, no flashes of light across its dark rocky bottom. That happens. Things feed on the brook trout in these pools: herons sometimes, maybe a bobcat or two. But they always regenerate. That's the way of nature. Two more pools, two and a half more fish. The half was a break-off because I didn't tie the hook with care. The old man taught me better than that.

I am older now and appreciate naps more than ever. When I was younger, I never napped. Now I take them when I can. That morning, after catching my six and one-half brookies, none more than eight inches long, each more valuable than any fish anywhere, I took a nap.....

He sat quietly beside me, trying not to disturb me, but I heard him anyway and looked up at him, sitting to my right, cleaning the fly line with his handkerchief.

"Well, well sleepy head. About time you woke up. Good heavens, you'll sleep your life away and miss all the fishin'. Thought I'd taught you better'n that. Shoot, go away for a while and the whole world goes to sleep on me. Pfft...."

"Pfft, yourself, old man. You used to nap too, as I recall."

"Yeah, I did. Still do too. But not when there's fish to be caught and flies to be dapped."

"Slow down... slow down, old man. We've got all day to fish." I slowed my speech way down. I wanted these minutes to last forever. "I haven't seen you since last year. Hold on and let's talk."

"Okay, what you want to talk about?"

"For one, how are things going?"

"What do you mean 'how are things going'? What kind of question is that to ask? Things are going like things always go. They go. Didn't I teach you nothin'? Or did you forget it all down there in the city?"

"No, I didn't forget. I remember...I remember," I replied.

We sat in silence for a few more minutes and I watched how he looked to the sky every so often, watching a red-tail hawk circle the top of Cagle's Knob.

"Lot more hawks these days," he declared.

"Yes. Farmers don't shoot them anymore. Getting rid of the DDT helps too," I answered, knowing the words weren't necessary.

"How are the wounds?" I asked.

"Oh, them - can't feel a thing. Best thing about this whole deal is the pain's finally gone. That and I get to fish some awfully nice water, alone if I want, and, if I need company, well there's always someone to fish with."

The old man had suffered for fifty years with the pain of a left shoulder patched back together after being greeted by a 7.92mm Sturmgewehr on a June morning in 1944 in the poetic sounding town of St. Mere-Eglise above a beach called Omaha. His knee was torn to shreds by shrapnel six months later at a small village called Bastogne. That one finally sent him home. The wounds were deep, the damage permanent, the pain ever-present. But he worked a job in town and ran his farm, alone after his wife died from the scarlet fever in '67, four years before he baptized me. I remember that night and waking the next morning in his house, all cried out, all the demons gone. On the wall across from my bed I saw his picture, framed and old, a young man in dress uniform, the light blue ribbon around his neck with thirteen white stars at the tie above the pendant, a silver parachute surrounded by wings and a silver glider, both pinned to his left breast.

I watched him get up from the ground beside me and walk to the edge of the rhododenron. He walked without a limp. Amazing! All the time I had known him, he had limped, until four years ago.

As he parted the rhododendron in front of him, he turned and winked at me. And then he disappeared, rod in right hand, on hands and knees into the leafy bushes, in pursuit of God's own gift.

I awoke. On the ground beside me was a single Lucky Strike, lit, with maybe a couple of puffs gone. I smiled. A wood duck hen whistled. The stream bubbled over rock fall and moss. A squirrel barked. I put out the cigarette, grabbed my backpack and rod, and began the walk back to the truck.

For the Colonel

A FATHER'S LOVE

SOMEWHERE in eastern North Carolina, I stopped to eat at one of those cinder-block walled barbeque joints that seem to pop up out of nowhere, near places like Jacksonville, Beaufort and Greenville. As the waitress placed the chopped pork plate in front of me, my cell phone rang. It was my wife. I knew immediately that something was wrong. My wife hates telephones; if she calls me, there is a problem at home. If she calls me when I'm out of town on business, something terrible has happened.

"Your father called. You need to go see him, Jack. He says he's dying."

I dropped a twenty on the table, along with the untouched pork, and left for Tennessee, the next few hours dribbling by beneath the drone tires rolling over milled concrete pavement, the seconds marked by the metronome of expansion joints. Just inside the Tennessee state line, a state trooper pulled me over. When I explained that my father was dying, he closed his book and told me to be careful and to follow him. He gave me a ninety miles per hour escort through the next two counties.

He looked older than I had imagined, my father. The white of the hospital room and the glare of the lights made him even paler than normal, with the broken capillaries of too many bottles of Old Crow etched across his wrinkled face like dendritic streams carving crevasses through craggy mountains. He was dying, the doctor said. A cancer was growing in his chest, liver and intestines. Surgery was not an option. It was only a matter of time. They offered a hospice. He chose to go home. I took him.

Two days later, he asked me to take him fishing. He said he'd watch me fish. He swore he was strong enough.

We drove past old haunts, old places where I had fished with him when I was a kid, back before he'd rediscovered the comfort that seemingly only a bottle of amber liquid could give him. When we came to the river, he moaned with every jostle and bump of the truck on the rutted hog path down to the water. I stopped several times; each time he assured me he was fine, each time he cursed me and told me to "get on with it." When we finally came to a stop, he spat blood on the grass as he exited the truck, pushing me away from helping him.

As I strung up my rod, I asked again if I could string him a rod.

"No Jack. My days of fishin', like most everythin' else, is done. I'm a' gonna sit up here and watch you, if you don't mind. I got this old polaroid here in case you get lucky and finally catch somethin'" He held up the Polaroid camera for me to see. His voice was so soft and weak that it cracked.

I fished. I caught some dinkers and then God in Heaven smiled and I caught a really good fish. I carried the good fish up the bank to let my father look at it and to touch it before I put it back in the water. Then we sat there and watched the water flow by, not saying a word, sharing the flask of bourbon, better bourbon than Old Crow, that I had slipped into my vest before leaving that morning.

On the way home he started talking. I pulled the truck over because his voice was so thin, I couldn't hear him over the din of the tires.

"You always was different, Jack. You couldn't stick around here. You go in the damn Army and you volunteer like an idiot to jump out of planes and do that stupid shit I told you not to do. Then you had to go off to college and get that damn degree like you was somebody. What the hell was you tryin' to prove?

You know, I always thought you was a damned fool for fishin' with that fly rod shit. I always thought you were tryin' to show off, to show me that you was better'n me. And I damned sure thought you was full of shit for lettin' your catch go. I always wondered why go to the trouble a'catchin' a fish if all you was goin' to do was to let it go? "

I didn't answer. I turned and faced the windshield and started the car back onto the road. He grabbed my elbow and told me to drive south, back towards a place we had lived for a while when I was a kid, before he started drinking and before my mother died and before my life changed forever.

He slept the hour and a half that it took to get there and awoke just as we entered the town. I stopped the truck at a diner on the far side of town, the diner that had been there when I was a kid and before my dad had taken up drinking instead of living. We had eaten there then: early morning breakfasts and late evening dinners before and after bird hunts and fishing trips.

"Do you remember this place?", I asked as we sat down in a booth still upholstered in naugahyde that probably had been there when John Kennedy was still alive, back when my family was still a family. I couldn't remember. Can naugahyde last thirty years?

"Yeah, I remember. I remember bringin' you here when you was just a pup. Remember those two setters we had...Jackson and Longstreet? Damn, they was some fine dogs".

"Yes sir, they were the two best dogs I've ever seen."

"Well, they weren't that damned good, but they were fine. Your mamma's daddy gave 'em to me. Only thing that man ever gave me that wasn't a lecture," he muttered as he sipped the hot coffee that a blue eye-shadowed waitress had set before him.

He sat silently for a time, not saying a thing, not acknowledging the plate of meat and vegetables the waitress lay before him. I picked at my plate and watched him. He did not look like he should be out of bed, but I was not going to argue with him.

Then he looked up and stared at me. His eyes, yellow with jaundice and watery-weak, locked onto mine.

"You never knew, Jack, about this place, about what

happened here?"

"Yeah. We ate here when I was a kid."

"Not that. I never told you. I promised your mother I would never tell you. But I'm about to make myself a liar to her again, God bless her."

He continued: "I knew about the two moonshiners up there on the Knob, Jack."

When I was ten years old, I had gone fishing alone up on Gentry's Knob. I had stumbled on two moonshiners and their still. They had beaten me black and blue and had threatened to kill my family if I told anyone what I had seen. Shortly thereafter, my mamma had sent me to live with my grandfather. I had never said a word about it and had refused to answer the questions my parents had asked about the bruises.

"You came home one day all bloody and bruised and told your mamma you'd been in a fight. But I knew them bruises you carried didn't come from a kid. I'd been enough fights to know what it looked like when a grown man beat on somebody. I knew that was no kid that had done that to you. It had to be a grown man, at least one grown man. But I didn't say anything because I didn't want your mamma to know. It was me that made your mamma send you off to your granddaddy."

"I asked around to try to find out who it was that did that to you, but all I got was 'mind your own business.' Then one night I was sittin' in this diner having a cup of coffee when I heard two shitheads talkin' loud about some kid they was lookin' for. It didn't take long for me to figure it was the two men who had beaten you up and it was you that they were looking to find. I expect they were worried about the trouble you could cause them and they had decided they needed to visit you again."

"I picked up the coffee pot off the hot plate on the counter and threw the coffee at the face of the one that was looking at me. I cracked the pot on the head of the other. Those old steel pots hurt more than glass ones. Anyhow, I kind of went crazy and over did it, kickin' and clawin' and hittin' em and all. The judge sent me to jail for fifteen days for destruction of property. Them two moonshiners got sent to federal prison up at Brushy Mountain. They was a warrant out for them for shooting at some Feds."

I stared at him. I had never known. I had assumed they had sent me to live with my grandfather because I couldn't get along anymore with my father. Sometimes... some things...you never know.

Two weeks later he died. I buried him where he had asked me to: at the National Cemetery in Chattanooga, beneath the limbs of a great oak tree that had been a youngster when Grant and Sherman had passed this way more than a hundred and thirty years before. He'd asked me to say the eulogy and I had tried. I had tried to say something about heroes and how sometimes we don't know who the heroes are in our lives until it's too late. But I cried and I sobbed and the words wouldn't come. My friend Eugene "Turtle" Wallace caught me when my knees buckled.

A few weeks passed by and I finally made an excuse to go

fishing. I drove to the river and got out of the SUV and opened the tailgate and put on my waders and my boots. I rigged up the rod and put on my vest and reached into a pocket to retrieve the metal fly box that held the wet flies I intended to use that afternoon.

I opened the metal fly box and inside the metal fly box, slipped between the lid and the flies, was a polaroid picture, the picture of me fighting the fish that I had caught while my dad had watched from the bank more than a month before. On the back of the picture was scrawled, in my father's hand, "My son. I am proud."

THE LUCKY ONE

THE TRUTH was that I had not been happy for some time. For the first time in our twenty- one year marriage, the strain was starting to show. After one of our more intense arguments, my wife had told me "Maybe you need to leave; you don't seem happy here."

Work was no relief – the construction market was wrecked and I struggled every day to find work for my employees. When I had sat down with my pastor to talk about how unhappy I was, he filled my ear with his own problems. I suppose that what happens when you wake up one day and find you're older than your preacher.

So I planned a retreat, a day off from life, a day on the river. The weather forecast called for one of those February days that make suffering through a Southern summer worth it - sunny, highs in the low 60's. The TVA release schedule promised "pulsing" all afternoon – one generator on for an hour then off for two – perfect conditions for this time of year.

Friday night, when I got home from work, my wife informed me that my teenage son was having a couple of friends over for a 'spend the night' thing and they wanted to go paintballing on Saturday morning. I wanted to scream something about what about my own plans, but I kept my mouth shut and remembered to be a father.

Saturday morning, I loaded up the three boys and took them to The Farm. It's not actually a farm, just fifty-five acres of woods and ridges I own east of town. We call it "The Farm" because I don't have a better imagination. They shot each other with paint balls until their bruises could take no more and we were back home by one.

I loaded the truck quickly and hit the road and an hour and a half later, I was there.

The Hiwassee – the river gets its name from the Cherokee who came to Tennessee in the mid-13th Century. After running the Creeks south to Georgia, the Cherokee set up shop and gave this river its name which roughly translates into English as "Meadow Place." That's what it is – a river set in a meadow that meanders to the larger Tennessee River.

The Hiwassee is big water, as big a trout stream as there is in the South. TVA dammed it in the 30's to generate electricity for the local folk. Before the dams, it was smallmouth water. My grandfather would get misty-eyed talking about the thousands of bronze backs that took to the fly. But the dams made the tailwater cold enough in the summers to support trout and it holds some big ones. The Tennessee state record brookie, 3 pounds 14 ounce, was caught in her waters in 1973. Now it is mostly brown and rainbow water, but an occasional smallmouth does show up. I caught one four years ago.

She entices you all along the road that parallels her from

east of the 411 turn-off until you come to Reliance. You can fish along these western runs, but the best fish are further on. Some never get past the area downstream from Reliance – the temptation is too strong, the water too beautiful, too promising. But, if you have the patience and the willpower, you keep driving, over Webb's Bridge, right at Robin's, and right again at what used to be Adams Fly Shop, before Adams died and the place was shuttered. Then to the top of the ridge and you see her – wide, two hundred yards wide, braided with shoals, boulders and ledges of quartzite some eight hundred million years old. You stop and hold your breath, staring at the diamonds of the sunlight dappling her waters below you. And then you drive down to the Bend.

The meat fishermen fish a mile further up, near the boat ramp where drift boats put in for the float down river. My friend Ronnie Hall was the first to put a drift boat on the HI, as it is called, back in the '70's. He started a trend. Anyway, the state stocks 10-inch rainbows and browns (teenies, we call them) up there and the meat boys come right behind like vacuum cleaners, taking their tax dollars home in coolers.

The first parking lot is at Big Bend which is named because the HI turns hard around a mountain about a mile downstream. From the parking lot down to Reliance, that portion of the HI is managed as trophy water. You can only keep two fourteen inch or longer fish. Most practice catch and release. Some break the law, as was evident by the two teenagers I saw putting a stringer of ten to twelve-inch 'bows into a cooler when I got out of my truck. The Hiwassee doesn't accommodate cell phone usage and Rangers are rare.

As I finished putting on my waders, a pickup truck pulled up behind me. The driver got out to pay his two-dollar parking fee at the honor depository.

"They stocked up at the dock at three", he said. "They put a whole truck load of ten-inchers up there. You ought to go up there to fish, buddy. These fish down here are too finicky."

I thanked him for the information and told him I might go up there after a bit, but I wanted to fish below the Stair-Steps first. He nodded, dropped his envelope in the slot and drove off.

The Stair-Steps are a series of quartzite ledges that cross the river about a quarter-mile's walk downstream from the parking lot. The river drops about four feet here and, when the water's right, brownies like to lie in the oxygenated water below the steps and feed on whatever floats by. I like fishing there, partly because it's a likely place to catch fish and partly because it's seldom crowded – the quarter-mile slog being beyond the hundred-yard limit of most fishermen. I hold to the belief that most folk will not walk more than a hundred yards from the parking lot to fish, particularly if there are woods between their cars and the water. I'm thankful for this, because it keeps some water private.

I fished the Steps down to the Island for an hour, catching six or seven teenies, all browns, all on a soft-hackle beadhead peacock, and then started thinking about the stockers upstream. I gave in to the temptation, thinking about supper and how good a couple of 'bows would taste after dark. So I walked back to the truck, climbed in and drove the mile or so upstream to the boat ramp. Sure enough, there were a dozen folks, spinning rods in hand and likely with corn on their hooks, catching pasty looking stockers. I turned the truck around and drove to the Trillium Trail pull off.

I call it the Trillium Trail. I don't know what its real name is or if it has a name. I found it in the mid-70's, back when I still used a spinning rod. In spring, when the weather's right, it is covered with trillium, a beautiful tri-lobed flower that's supposed to be endangered. It may be endangered elsewhere, but not here – they blanket the ground like snow in spring. But the trillium, which was of course dormant in February, gives way to a thicket of Privet, evidence of white man's introduction of a European weed.

I had an hour until sunset. The water was cold – 47 degrees, the air warm – 60 degrees. The sun was working its way towards sinking behind the mountains. I worked the soft hackle peacock with no luck and then spotted a large pod of flashing fish, nymphing upstream from where I stood, gathered in a pothole.

I changed flies, thinking "midge" and put on a brassie, size 18 - nothing. I decided to try something else. While I stood there, facing upstream in the water, opening my fly box, I saw something flash to my right. At first I thought maybe it was just a submerged leaf. But then I saw it move again, a flash of amber light in the sunlit water. It was a big flash - a very big flash. My heartbeat picked up a stroke or two. I thought: how do I get to that fish?

There was a trough in front of me and then a ledge covered with maybe six inches of water. The trough looked deep, maybe six feet or so (I should know by now – I've fallen into it a couple of times in past years). The fish was holding in a pocket on the other side of the ledge. This presented a problem – the fish was 45 feet away with both fast and slow water between us. How to drift a nymph across this without the bellied line in the fast water yanking the nymph out of the pocket where the fish was?

I knew I would only have one, maybe two casts and drifts before I spooked the fish. I'm not the most accomplished caster – the "slack line cast" has never been my strong suit – but there was no way I could get better position without spooking the fish or taking a dunking, so I had to take my chances.

A friend of mine says, "Sometimes you eat the bear and sometimes the bear eats you" – that day I ate the bear. I tied on a fly I had created the night before, while goofing off at the vice. I called it "LaFontaine's Serendipity" - a mongrelization of Gary LaFontaine's Caddis Nymph and Craig Matthew's Serendipity. I tied it Olive, with Olive Hare Dubbing, weighted, segmented with thin olive tubing and with a trimmed deer hair thorax. I knew the fly would have to get down in a hurry, so I mashed three split shot onto the leader and prayed for gravity.

I cast a quarter upstream, rolling the rod to put the "esses" into the line so that drag wouldn't grab the nymph right away. The nymph landed long, but the water pulled it directly into the lane I hoped for. "Now, if only the bug will sink fast enough", I thought, as I saw the red "Amnesia" leader butt section pass over the fish. I thought I saw the fish roll and was worried for a second that I might have spooked him. Then I saw the "Amnesia" twitch. I raised the rod tip, hoping against hope that the line or hook hadn't caught on a submerged rock. No! Fish On!

He did a stupid thing, for such a big fish – he turned and headed downstream. Trout don't breathe well when their heads are not facing the water flow – water needs to flow through their gills and this is best done facing the current. Fish that head downstream tire in a hurry. But my boy headed down. I turned, keeping the rod held high, trying to keep the leader from abrading on the submerged rocks. Quartzite, besides being one of the hardest rocks on the planet, has an aggravating tendency to form knife-sharp edges and it will cut a leader like soft cheese.

The fish turned left, the tip of my rod flipping with the move. I adjusted and saw him disappear beneath a ledge. I had to get him out of there or the line would be cut or entangled. I tried to move towards him and downstream, but the trough got in my way. Before I could stop, I was sliding down an angled rock face and water was coming in over my waders. I shuddered at the rush of cold water and knew it was baptism time. Then, miraculously, my right foot felt a crease and I stepped up, back to waist deep water.

My floundering had somehow been transmitted to the fish that then turned back, away from his hole and into the channel where I had found him. He bore upstream, pulling hard. For one of the rare times in my life of fishing for trout in the Southeast, I actually had to use the drag on my reel – palming would not work.

Eventually I turned him and worked him towards me slowly, working to keep him sideways to the current. I stepped back towards shore, back on a gravel bottom with the water mid-calf deep. The fish ran and retreated, but with each run, the spurts were shorter. I could see him now - the biggest trout I've caught in Tennessee. He was too big for the small net I carried – a good four inches longer than the length of my forearm from elbow to fingertips, maybe twenty two inches long and with full girth. Beautiful! The deepest golden belly – that was the flash I'd seen when he'd been dining in his restaurant, before he ordered from my menu.

For a few seconds, as I brought him to hand, the thought struck me that I should get him mounted. I had no camera with me and no one would believe the story when I told it. But I remembered, really I did remember – it's funny what things go through your mind and how many things can go through your mind over just a few seconds – why I had come to the HI. I was unhappy and looking to find happiness. That brownie deserved happiness too, whatever happiness to a fish is. I certainly knew that he wouldn't find happiness hanging on my wall, nor, eventually, after the newness wore off, would I. So I snipped the hook from his lip and held him for a minute, facing upstream. Slowly he started to move again and then, in a flash, he was gone.

I walked back through the woods to my truck and put up my gear, pouring the water out of my waders and feeling really cold for the first time. The heater warmed and I started down the river road, headed for home. It was six thirty and the sun was almost gone, only the last rays of light still keeping the world alight.

I was thinking about the fish and thinking how old I was and how cold I was. I cursed myself for my clumsiness and my forgetfulness in not bringing my wading staff. I started to curse the HI for being such a difficult place to wade with its knife-edged ledges and its deep, narrow troughs and its too-finicky fish. But then I looked up and saw through the windshield two teenage boys who were fishing with spinning rods and who were clad only in t-shirts and in wet-to-the-crotch blue jeans. They were standing in forty-seven degree water and were having the time of their lives. And I saw myself standing where those boys were standing, only four decades earlier, when I was a boy and the possibilities of life and the pure fun of being free on a river were all that I needed and none of the noises of life ever got in the way of enjoying where I was.

I stopped the truck, got out, and watched those boys fish. I lit a cigar and as I smoked it, the words came to me:

Why are you unhappy? Look around yourself. Think of your family. You have it all.

I was filled with that feeling that starts somewhere deep in your soul and grows in an instant to where your hair stands up on the back of your neck and your skin tingles and somewhere between your heart and your brain and your gut, you feel an awakening and you know, YOU KNOW, that God is talking to you.

I said a prayer and thanked God for the day and for the fish and for the lesson the boys had given me and for my family. Then I started the truck and turned on the radio. A station from Chattanooga came over the speakers with a song by Ms. Allison Krause and Union Station: *The Lucky One*.

Karma.

Two hours later, I walked into my house. My wife came into the kitchen and stood beside me and looked up at me. I turned to her and opened my arms and she stepped into them. We held each other. My son walked in, saw us, and turned and walked back into the family room. My wife still held me. I heard the kids laughing in the living room.

I said a second prayer of thanks.

For Susan

And a great and strong wind was rending the mountains and breaking in pieces the rocks before the Lord; but the Lord was not in the wind.

And after the wind, an earthquake, but the Lord was not in the earthquake.

And after the earthquake, a fire, but the Lord was not in the fire.

And after the fire, a sound of gentle whisper...

"What are you doing here?"

ABOUT THE AUTHOR

D. L. Gilmore is a sometime fly fisherman, sometime woodworker, occasional writer, most of the time registered professional civil engineer and full-time husband, father, brother, and friend. He served the Republic for seven years as a combat engineer with the United States Army, including three years as a member of the 101st Airborne Division. He is a graduate of the Georgia Institute of Technology, a founder of the Soggy Sweat Society of Whiskey and Whisky Lovers, and a founding member of the Gathering of the Clan Fly Fishing club. He owns a kilt and shares his truck with his dog Jette, a Deutsche Drathaar.

He lives in Northwest Georgia at the head of a lovely valley that is lined with limestone streams and that stretches northward through East Tennessee and western Virginia and into Pennsylvania. He believes in God, America, and Nature.

www.ingramcontent.com/pod-product-compliance
Lightning Source LLC
Chambersburg PA
CBHW020614250626
47154CB00004B/1514